First Edition
Published 2018

Copyright © Stannington Library Writers Group 2018

The authors have asserted their moral rights in accordance
with Copyright, Designs and Patents Act 1988

ISBN:9781719896696

Contents

Preface

This is a collection of short stories by members of Stannington Library Writers' Group. The group encourages writers to get together to discuss their work and obtain peer critique. We are informal and open to all genres and experience levels.

If you would like to join us, please come along. The first meeting is free. We meet in Stannington Library on Uppergate Road, Stannington, Sheffield, UK at 1:00pm on the first Saturday of each month. Email us at the address below for more information.

This book contains contributions from eight of our members. We hope you enjoy reading our work. Other anthologies published by our group are: 1stannthology, nXstannthology, ChristmasAnthology2016 and ChristmasAnthology2017, all available from Amazon. Proceeds from all our anthologies go towards the upkeep of the library where we meet.

Please email us with feedback, good or bad, as receiving honest critique is the best way to improve as a writer.

Email stanningtonwriters@gmail.com.

Three Folk Tales

(Based on oral myths and legends)

Wise Woman of the Dreamtime

(Australia)

Carol Ritson

Long, long ago, the female ancestor wandered this red earth harvesting sweet potatoes. As she searched for a waterhole, an evil Red Back Spider - whose spirit could change into any animal, and then, by pretending to be their friend, would trap and eat them - appeared in the form of the male ancestor. It tried to befriend the female ancestor by promising to teach her where the water holes were, but then began to lead her away in the wrong direction. Luckily, the deity of water, the Rainbow Serpent, who had been watching the whole event unfolding, leapt out of his waterhole into the sky and landed at the female ancestor's feet. The female ancestor, knowing that the rainbow across the sky created by the serpent would lead her directly to the source of water, realised that the male ancestor must be, in fact, the evil lying spider and demanded it to return to his original form. When it had, the Rainbow Serpent leaped back into the waterhole and then across the landscape from one waterhole to the next, to the next, making rainbows across the earth.

This is how women became wise and gained the knowledge of water within the landscape.

Wayfinders

(Polynesia)

Carol Ritson

Many moons ago, an anchored boat gently rocked upon the shallow water. On the shore, the community danced frantically around the fire, eating, drinking, celebrating; everyone was gathered. As the morning sun rose over the horizon, the newly-wed couple kissed their loved ones goodbye and stepped into the boat. They took nothing with them. No food, no presents, no clothing, no oars, just a fish hook, a cooking pan and a small container of water. They set off on their new adventure. Where would it end? The decision was in the hands of the wind and the water, but with the many thousands of islands around, they were bound to stumble upon one fairly quickly. For two days they drifted across the open blue water. Suddenly, a new and distant island came into view. Paddling with their hands they landed upon the shore. 'The Fathers' had predicted "Able" while 'The Mothers' "Shorma" - either would be ideal. From the look of the island, with its high central hill covered in woodland, it seemed that 'The Fathers' were correct. "Able" was fabled not only for its many varied plants, small animals, trees for whittling wood into tools and for building shelters, but also for its great marine life, so there was fish aplenty.

They were happy, grateful and content in the knowledge that the wind had delivered them safely to a fruitful and plentiful place that would be perfect to start their marriage and bring forth future new lives.

Warrior Women

(Hebrides, Scotland)

Carol Ritson

Once, in ancient times, some travellers arrived on the island, drawn there by the incredibly useful bloodstone. It was a rock which could be shaped into tools in a similar way to flint. The men had grown up with the legend of the island, of the 'large, powerful warrior women who had once lived on the great volcanic outcrop that brooded over the skyline.' It was said that they 'welcomed all uninvited guests with bloody violence, destroying and burning their bodies.' The downfall of the women, the travellers decided, was due to female stupidity and ignorance. For the legend concluded by stating that 'as the bodies burned on the women's fires, directly above them, high in the sky, a flurry of unworldly beguiling lights started to flicker and dance. As the ribbons weaved their way towards the shore, the warrior women became entranced by them. They followed them, wading deeper and deeper into the water until they had all drowned.' The travellers, therefore, concluded that the island no longer posed a risk to life. Their treasure would be collected, and swiftly brought home where they would live long, and prosperous lives. The first two days went perfectly, the lookouts at the base of the outcrop saw no one and the rock was plentiful. But as the third night drew in, the clouds menacingly covered the sky, and the lookouts never returned. Several fires were spotted in the distance. The lights started to dance and flicker faintly in the sky towards them. The cloud cover lifted. The sky became ablaze with colour until its brightness revealed that they were surrounded by a fully equipped army of warrior women, dressed for battle.

And they realised that no one had ever returned home from this place, to retell the legend of the island correctly.

Clarissa's Party

Penny Wragg

"More champers darling?"

I hear Roddy's voice echoing down the years. Glasses were filled and refilled. Clarissa had a fit of the giggles. She was a bubbly girl. Champagne suited her. She'd bought a gorgeous new frock for the New Year party - strapless with a full skirt, a petticoat underneath, slim cream court shoes on her dainty little feet. Looking back at the photo now, I'm struck by her resemblance to Audrey Hepburn.

I remember that the weather that New Year's Eve was uncommonly mild which is how we came to be outside in the garden. That was what threw me at first when I found the photo at the bottom of a tatty old cardboard box.

Janie was there, lolling carelessly against a tree, wearing a sort of soft flowing chiffon number in pale green. She had a rather aristocratic bearing and a long graceful neck. She was always a calming presence in our set, not quite as giddy as the rest of us, yet still joining in with our antics.

Pippa was there, full of energy, pretty and petite, always laughing and thinking of the next possible practical joke. I think it was she who persuaded Nigel to go up the tree and lie there balancing precariously on a branch with a cushion under his head. Dear old Nigel!

And Roddy, of course, was in charge of the bottle, making sure everyone was alright, so courteous and polite.

Where was I? I was the one behind the camera. My father had lent it to me to capture the occasion.

Clarissa's party was one of many. We were "the gang". We partied at every opportunity - birthdays, Christmas, New Year,

7

summer, or just when we felt like it. We were all in our early twenties at the time of this picture. Some, like Clarissa, looked younger. She certainly acted it! Others, like Roddy, looked older and acted more responsibly. This image captures a moment which appears carefree, fun-filled; friends looking forward to a future which held hope and promise.

Clarissa was, of course, destined to go into the fashion industry. She was a successful designer for many years, creating wonderful wedding dresses for famous people.

Roddy went into banking and became steady and conventional as we expected he would.

Nigel inherited a stately home from his great uncle and worked very hard to restore it and eventually open it up to the public. The house and gardens now belong to the National Trust.

Pippa loved dancing and formed her own dance group. I think they even appeared on "Top of the Pops."

Janie, to our surprise, went abroad with a Christian charity to help people in a very poor area, I forget where. There was little clean water or sanitation. She helped to build a health centre and a school. She had a real rapport with the children which seemed to compensate a bit for her not being able to have any of her own. We were all devastated when we heard that she'd been struck down by a rare tropical disease and died at the age of 35.

The rest of us tried to carry on and keep in touch but the loss of dear Janie left a huge gap. The last time the remaining five of us were together was at Roddy's wedding. He married a girl he'd known for ages through work. I never thought of him as anxious or highly strung, so it was a tremendous shock to hear that he'd shot himself when he got into financial difficulties. I was abroad at the time and couldn't go to his funeral.

Nigel and Pippa kept in touch with me but about fifteen years ago Nigel had a terrible accident falling off a roof. We never knew whether it was a prank gone wrong or whether he was doing repairs to the manor house. I tend to think the former as he always had a reckless streak.

Pippa was inconsolable. She'd always remained close friends with him. Much of her spark disappeared and she became obsessive about exercise and her classical ballet training, losing so much weight that she struggled with anorexia, dying a few years after Nigel.

Clarissa and I carried on having parties but with only the two of us left from the old crowd things were never the same. We never had quite as much fun with our newer friends.

One morning I opened my newspaper and there was a headline about Clarissa. She had mysteriously disappeared. That was six years ago now. There's been no trace of her according to the police. Who knows what happened to her?

Well - I do actually. She was my wife for several years. She was never easy to live with. She kept cheating on me. I'm afraid after a while I snapped. I've disposed of her body pretty well I think. My secret's safe and will die with me. I don't know why I kept this photo. I tend to get sentimental, particularly at New Year. I think now it's time to get rid of it and let the past go. I've remarried and we're very happy together, for now at least. She's just coming into the room.

"More champers darling?"

After the Earthquake

Penny Wragg

A group of writers are stuck in a room together following an earthquake...

Jo opened her eyes slowly. Her eyelashes were clogged with dust. Heavens, she was covered in the stuff! She was on the floor surrounded by rubble. It was dark but there was a chink of light showing from somewhere. What on earth had happened? One minute she was watching a quidditch match, the next she was here...where though? Panic rose as bile in her throat. What would Cormoran Strike do? What would Harry do? Get it together woman. Just then something scuttled out of a corner and across the floor in front of her. She must be delirious. It was wearing a little red coat and hat.

"So sorry dear," said a female voice from the far corner of the room.

"You must have tapped into my imagination. I always think of animals wearing clothes."

A kindly-looking weather beaten lady wearing outdoor clothes and carrying a shepherd's crook materialized in front of Jo, having obviously crawled over. She extended a hand.

"Mrs Heelis, sheep farmer. You might know me better as Beatrix."

"Pleased to meet you. I have no idea how I got here."

"Nor me but I'm sure there's a rational explanation," replied Beatrix.

Another voice joined the conversation saying in a posh upper-class accent: "Hello there! I'm Dame Agatha. In my experience we must look for clues and use our 'little grey cells' as my creation dear Hercule would say. We should also use our intuition and observation as dear Jane would do. Now let's have a look around. Unfortunately we are slightly hampered. We will have to crawl on our hands and knees. Be careful...oh! Oh damnation! My hand's caught in something."

Jo couldn't help giggling when she noticed what had happened.

"It's a mousetrap!" Dame Agatha wasn't at all amused, but Beatrix saw the funny side of it.

"There must be a dear little mouse family living here. I can just imagine their little outfits."

"Come over to the light," said Jo, examining Agatha's hand. Then she gave a start. "Does anyone know who that is sitting in the shadows?" She pointed to a small still man wearing a sort of turban and robes. He had his legs crossed and an expression of peace on his face.

"The wound is the place where the light enters you." *(1)*

The three ladies were still. There was a calming presence about this man. "Who are you?" asked Agatha, trying not to interrogate.

"My name is a long complicated one, but usually I'm known as Rumi. I'm a Persian poet and mystic."

"You must have died a long time ago," replied Agatha accusingly.

"In earthly terms, yes, in 1273, but really do poets ever die?"

No one could find an answer to this.

Then from another corner of the room came a melancholy disembodied voice.

"For oft when on this couch I lie, in vacant or in pensive mood, they flash upon that inward eye which is the bliss of solitude......" *(2)*

"Oh, for heaven's sake!" thought Jo. "I have to be shacked up with my least favourite poet - Wordsworth!"

As they approached the voice, a figure dressed in velvet knickerbockers and frilly shirt came into view, lying on a couch. Both man and couch were covered in dust. He seemed to be in a world of his own, not really noticing his surroundings. They silently agreed to leave him to his musings - for now.

Suddenly a loud shout punctured their thoughts.

"Ay up! What's goin' on 'ere then? Who do I spy? I'm trapped in a building and there's dust in mi eye. I'm Ian. I'm the Barnsley Bard. I write poems and party hard."

A stocky bespectacled sixty something chap climbed through a hole and waved cheerfully.

"Do you always speak in rhyme?" asked Jo.

"Aye lass, don't think it is a curse. There are worse ways to speak than in verse. And the last thing I want from thee is pity when I turn everything into a ditty."

"I can see that Ian's going to be really annoying," muttered Jo to herself.

Agatha was determined to bring some order to the chaos.

"Look, let's set about this in a logical manner. We need to ascertain *how* we all got here, indeed *where* we are, and *why?* Have we got anything to eat or drink to keep our strength up?"

"Hello there!" shouted a cheerful female voice. A dark-haired woman climbed into the room through a hole in the floorboards.

"What an adventure! Jolly hockey sticks! Don't worry, I've bought a huge picnic basket with potted meat sandwiches and lashings of lemonade."

Jo sighed. Could it get any worse? "Am I right in thinking you're Enid? I don't suppose you've got a map showing us where the treasure is buried have you?"

Enid's mood changed. "Yes, I'm Enid and there's no need to be sarcastic. Why would I have a treasure map in the middle of an earthquake?"

"Sorry," Jo replied. "I think we're all a little bit anxious."

Unseen by the others, Mr Wordsworth had stirred from his couch and cautiously approached the group.

"Perchance I have discovered some Grasmere gingerbread in my pocket which I will happily share if it will bestow pleasure. It is a special secret recipe."

The others thanked him warmly and Jo resolved to be kind to him. Surprisingly, Beatrix produced some salad although she warned against eating too much lettuce as it "could make one rather soporific."

Things got even better when it was revealed that Ian had a Denby Dale pie in his haversack. He presented it thus:

"It's a symphony of crust, tatties, gravy and meat. A Denby Dale pie makes your life complete." *(3)*

They all tucked into this impromptu feast, with the exception of Rumi, who declared that for him spiritual food would suffice.

As they talked they came to the conclusion that they weren't at all sure how they had arrived here. It was a sudden transportation from beside the lake, the quidditch field, the moors, their study, a secret island, or a pub in Yorkshire. Rumi had been sitting meditating under a tree although he couldn't remember where. Neither did they know where they were - a ruined building somewhere in the aftermath of an earthquake. The "why" didn't even matter. They just wanted to survive.

After their meal, they tried to make themselves as comfortable as possible for the night. Mr Wordsworth graciously let Beatrix and Agatha sleep on his couch whilst he lay his head on Rumi's lap. Ian fell asleep straightaway as he was so full of pie, and his snores were destined to keep most of the assembled company awake all night. Jo thought that they might precipitate another earthquake. Enid had packed up the picnic basket but was now quite restless. Jo was disappointed. Enid had turned out to be more volatile than she expected, and she had even admitted to not liking children very much!

Ian was first to wake in the morning. Well, he'd had the best night's sleep of all of them! His exclamation: "Oh 'eck, ah'll go tut foot of our stairs!" soon woke the others. He was even too shocked to find a rhyme. He was looking at a heap of clothes in the middle of the

14

room. But no… "Stand back," yelled Agatha, "Don't touch the corpse!" Rumi said that he could bestow a blessing on the deceased person from a distance. Everyone thought that Agatha was becoming rather bossy as she took out a notebook from her pocket and proceeded to ask them each in turn if they had an alibi for the previous night. Realizing the foolishness of this, she then asked if anyone recognized the deceased. Everyone remained silent although Jo and Ian exchanged a knowing look.

They were all startled when an elderly gentleman appeared through a gap in the rubble. He was about eighty years old and had a distinguished air about him. He carried himself in a manner which commanded respect.

"Who are you?" asked Beatrix.

"I can't tell you just now I'm afraid. I'm working undercover," was his reply.

"Are you a spy?" asked Jo.

"Yes," he whispered, "I've just come in from the cold."

To the group as a whole he announced, "It's extremely important that you refrain from doing or saying anything which may jeopardize your chance of escape. Don't react to finding this body. Try to forget it's there."

Rumi said quietly: "Out beyond ideas of wrongdoing and rightdoing there is a field. I'll meet you there." *(4)*

Mr Wordsworth had a tear in his eye as he patted Rumi on the shoulder and confessed to how much he was missing the daffodils. Everyone else felt a bit awkward. The spy ("Call me David") left abruptly the way he'd come. Ian took Jo to one side. "Do you think…….?" He began.

Jo nodded. "Yes, I'm not sure which, but it's either Ant or Dec."

Agatha and Enid had crept up behind them. "There's something odd about this body," said Agatha, arms folded decisively across her chest. "You may think I'm old fashioned," said Enid, "but I think it's a trick. I suspect it's CGI, you know computer generated." And with that she walked right through it.

"If that's not real," said Jo, "is any of this?"

"If I may pose a question" interjected Rumi quietly. "What is reality? Does it come from within each one of us or are we part of a higher spiritual quest?"

"There is summat in what tha's said," replied Ian, "But it's gonna give me a pain in mi 'ead."

Suddenly the spy ("Call me David") appeared again. "Listen, there's not much time. Sit down in a circle and join hands. You're going to hear an announcement. It may come as a shock."

They all felt Rumi's presence become very powerful.

"We need to make sure that the bonds between us are strong."

"There's summat in that or I'll eat mi 'at," muttered Ian. Then they fell silent.

There was a crackle, then a voice which some of them recognized.

"Hello earthquake survivors. This is Davina here. It's time for one of you to be evicted from the ruins."

They looked at each other and instinctively knew that they all felt the same. Jo became spokeswoman.

"No Davina. We're not doing it. No one is leaving. We belong together."

"Well done," said David the spy. "Listen Davina. I worked it all out. I know about your grubby little so-called reality show."

Ian became excited, or as excited as possible without a pint in his hand.

"We're going to challenge the banality of your reality!"

"Yay!" they all shouted, or the equivalent according to their lifestyle.

16

At this point, Davina sounded as if she had lost a little bit of composure. "I'll just have a word with the producer...," they heard her say, and then almost tearfully, "this is live TV you know and it is my livelihood."

"Listen everyone at Channel Five," said David. "You've overstretched yourselves this time. You've messed about with the Earth's structure by manufacturing an earthquake and in your usual inept way you've initiated a time shift. This means that Rumi can converse with Ian, and Beatrix can talk to Jo, and William Wordsworth has now met Agatha and Enid. ("What bliss," sighed Mr Wordsworth)

"Be with those who help your being," said Rumi, quoting himself. *(5)*

"It will all be in my report to MI6," said David. They could tell that Davina and the producer were now hysterical. Beatrix had been very quiet but now she rose to the challenge.

"We are all famous writers of our times. We are all in possession of powerful imaginations. I propose that we harness this power to overcome reality shows once and for all. We can bring our imagined creations to life here and now."

Davina was now a gibbering wreck. "I'm finished! I'm finished!"

On television screens all over the world, people watched entranced as a new picture appeared before them. They saw a beautiful lakeside scene where a "host of golden daffodils" swayed gently in the wind. They saw a garden filled with the most perfect vegetables they'd ever seen. Peter Rabbit was sitting contentedly munching lettuce and carrots with Flopsy, Mopsy and Cottontail. Mr McGregor didn't mind. He was on his way to the pub and soon found himself eating pie and drinking beer with Hercule Poirot, Professor Dumbledore, and all the Famous Five, although the latter were only drinking lemonade. Even Timmy the dog was allowed in. Above them was a banner which read "Welcome to Barnsley".

"We've found the treasure after all," exclaimed Julian, "It's Barnsley!"

Next the camera panned to a very pretty sitting room where Jane Marple was knitting a scarf and taking tea with George Smiley, who kept smiling at her comments enigmatically. Everyone was happy.

Everyone was spiritually connected to each other, just as Rumi had always known they would be.

As the worlds of fact and fiction began to collide, the camera crew just escaped in time to join the others in the pub before Harry Potter appeared, waved his wand, and shouted "Expelliarmus!" The whole worldwide television network was obliterated. Nobody missed it.

With grateful thanks to Enid Blyton, Agatha Christie, John Le Carre (David Cornwell), Ian McMillan, Beatrix Potter, J.K.Rowling, Jalaloddin Mohammed Balkhi Rumi, and William Wordsworth for their contribution to literature.

References

1. *Rumi quotes- www.goodreads.com*

2. *William Wordsworth "Daffodils" 1807.*

3. *Part of the Denby Dale Pie Poem (or Piem) written by Ian McMillan for National Pie Week 2012. YouTube.*

4. *The Essential Rumi (1995) translated by Coleman Barks.*

5. *Be with those… poem by Rumi www.poemhunter.com*

STANNINGTON NOIR: You Don't Need a Weatherman to Know Which Way the Wind Blows

Bob Mynors

Apartment on ground floor. Garden apartment. City high-rise. 'Piece of cake.' Bedroom window - fastened from inside. Living room window - same. More windows on side of building. Small one to living room - same. 'No worry.' Kitchen window open very slightly. 'Praise be for extractor fans that don't work.' Pull. No response. Subtle shake once, twice - slightly more vigorously. Free on third try. 'Useless security.' Brute force would have done it ... 'but who needs it when the jerk makes it this easy.' In through open window. Knock over junk on window sill. Shit! Mostly cleaning stuff, but – aw no - glass jar with nails and screws and whatever. Not any longer. All over kitchen floor. Pick up, every last bit. Return all to window sill. Nearly same as mess seen from outside. No reaction from other apartments. 'Good sound-proofing these places.' Step into living room. No clues. Nothing unusual. Except ... bedclothes folded and stacked at end of pull-out sofa. A pull-out. 'Sleeps in here then.' Switch search to bedroom. Office. Desk. Computer. One, two - four file cabinets. Best start in those. 'No .... not seen one of those for long enough.' Small square zip-fastened carry-case for CDs on desk. 'Dope.' Rank amateur. 'Too easy.' Quick look inside case. Yep. 'That's the stuff.' Into bag. Head for front door. Straight outside. Not gonna use public areas inside block

From the privacy of her office loo, PI Tia Plenty heard an alto saxophone rip the air. Earl Bostic's *Harlem Nocturne*. It was her business ringtone. She'd not heard it for days. Business was pretty thin for UrbanAgriTecs right now. And here she was – in no position to pick up the call. Two minutes later, phone in newly-washed hand, she checked her call log. "Private number. Typical." *Private number* could mean anything - new corporate client maybe. Someone hassling for a bill to be paid just as likely. More likely. It hardly mattered which, unless someone rang back. "Oh, ring back, why don't you?" Almost on cue, Earl Bostic blared out again. Not for long this time. "Good morning. UrbanAgriTecs. PI Tia Plenty speaking." After what, for her, was an all too customary pause, she went on to say, "Plenty. Tia Plenty. It's my name. Tia is short for Sebastia which is the name my parents gave to me. Plenty is the name I inherited from them."

After a further pause, she said, "Yes, we do offer a confidential investigation service, but the area we specialise in is animals. Animals with a commercial value, generally - livestock, working animals, show animals. From time to time, we get someone with a pet and a perfect pedigree. Realistically, that means any creature whose owner thinks it worth laying down hard cash on insurance, either against theft or against some other loss. I'm not sure we can offer the kind of expertise that you …"

Tia paused again. She listened to a tale coming at her down the phone. Eventually she responded. "I'm sure you're right. I don't imagine there are many agencies specialising in theft of art works and climate change data. Not at the same time. Certainly not in this city. It sounds a pretty niche sort of crime, if I'm honest. But I'm a detective, so I can't afford to go making wild assumptions. About anything."

After what proved her final pause of the conversation, she said, "Yes I do know where the library is – in the park. In there then - about forty-five minutes. And you're sure I can get coffee there?"

Almost exactly on time, Tia pulled into the car park by the recycling bins. She knew this area. She'd worked here before. It was a pretty little place. The library was as small and as smart as any you could ask for. As she walked inside, she saw the coffee machine in the far corner, and sitting at a table next to it she saw a young man reading a newspaper, looking just the way she had known he would – black t-shirt, denim jacket, hair in need of a trim. Even though he was seated, she could tell he would be no taller than she was. It was a surprise then when the voice that greeted her came from behind

"Hello. You must be Ms Plenty. I'm sorry I wasn't here when you arrived."

The voice belonged to an all together more striking figure than she had imagined. More striking than the scruffy lad reading the paper, that was for sure. This one was taller that she had expected, and older, and he was wearing a blue suit. No tie but a smart suit. "Good morning. Yes. I'm Tia Plenty, UrbanAgriTecs," and she held out her hand. "It's you I just spoke to on the phone?"

"Good morning. Yes. I'm Harrison Richardson." He handed her a card, which made Tia smile a little at a name she felt was almost as ridiculous as her own. She also noted how firm and how warm his handshake was as he asked, "How do you take your coffee?"

Over cappuccinos in over-size mugs with big white spots, he told his story and she listened. He had been robbed, burgled, though not a standard domestic burglary. What few possessions he said he had were left undisturbed, it seemed, and the thieves had identified and taken the only thing he did have that had any real value. They had taken data – weather data that somehow got transformed in art. Tia did not understand. The data was stored on encrypted CDs, and it was these CDs that had been stolen, in their carrying case. The data had no real commercial value, he explained, though it did provide him with a modest income source - through the artwork, but its significance was much wider

"OK. I'll start with all the obvious questions, if I may – and please don't feel patronised or like I'm not taking you seriously. It's just that we need some ground rules here, and I need to know what the ground is like."

"I understand, Ms Plenty. I promise I won't feel patronised."

"And before we start, can I ask you to drop the *Ms Plenty*?" She felt she was being a little forward, dropping her normal professional distance so soon. Usually she preferred to stand back from her clients, at least till she felt they done something to deserve her confidence. But it felt right this time. "It never sounds like me. Please - call me Tia, or even just T. Most people do." As she said this, she saw him raise an eyebrow, slightly but quite definitely, so she added, "Yes. That's right. T. Just *T* on its own. No milk or sugar."

Smiling a broad, warm smile, he said, "I know how you feel. I'm saddled with two surnames and they wouldn't work well together even if they were hyphenated. In fact, lots of people refuse to believe they aren't. There's no obvious front door to them either. I answer to many things, but Harry has always seemed the simplest option. So, please call me Harry."

"Harry. Right. I'm glad we've got that sorted. Here come the obvious questions then. How secure is your encryption? What the hell are you doing keeping sensitive data on CDs, not locking it down on a server somewhere? And have you reported the theft to the police?"

He had said he would not feel patronised but couldn't help feeling a little hurt. This woman he had never met before and who knew nothing of his work was making a lot more sense than he felt he had done in the last twenty-four hours. "Good questions," he told her, "and I'll try to come up with good answers. Encryption first. It's as good as I can make it. I use some pretty high-end software and I update very frequently, like every few days. I'm not even going to name the software because you've probably never heard of it and you really don't need to know, but it is good. Take it from me, it is way beyond industry standard. But it's not the data being accessed that bothers me. It's the loss of it, the destruction of it perhaps."

"What sort of data is it?"

"Nothing particularly controversial. Just climate data from around the world. The sort of stuff anybody can get hold of, provided they pay. It can be replaced easily too, most of it. It would cost but there would be no problem getting hold of it. But I don't think they want the data for itself. I think they just want me not to have it."

"You'll have to explain that one to me, Harry. What's so special about you, if you don't mind me asking, that someone would bother taking all the risks involved in carrying out a burglary just to stop you doing whatever it is you do?" After initially being very impressed by Mr Harrison Richardson, Tia was beginning wonder about him. The deliberately wacky business card - how she hated that word, but it seemed to be the only appropriate one here – with its not-as-witty-as-it-wanted-to-be email address. Email addresses like that don't just happen. (forkassed@gmail.com – it took her a moment, but she'd got it. How long must he have spent making that one up?) And the strapline – *can we have our weather back please, mister?* He had a sense of humour, obviously. But humour in the workplace could often be a cover for something sinister. And was it a strapline or was it a mission statement? For all the man's English charm, the humour sounded straight out of Silicon Valley. So what was he trying to achieve with it all? He was starting to come across like a man with a mission, and they could be hard work

"It's complicated."

"I should hope so. It's a matter of professional pride to think people never bring me the easy cases these days." She shot him a friendly smile which he returned. He'd realised she wasn't being entirely serious

"It's just that I've got two things going on really. I'm a climate activist and I'm a climate artist. The first really gets up a lot of people's noses, but the other - people seem to love it. Enough people. The money I earn from the art funds the activism. There's a hashtag.weatherman – that's what we call ourselves - in the US and one in Denmark and one in India. And the one in Denmark is actually a hashtag.weatherwoman. We're a very right-on team."

"I would never have doubted that for a moment, but you'll still have to run a couple of those things by me again. Climate activist I think I understand, and I'm not going to ask too much about it because I'm sure we'd quickly run into behaviour that might be ever so slightly illegal, or at least anti-social. And I think I don't need to know about that."

Very quietly, almost mouthing the words, he said, "You don't. Not really. It's a positive thing, all about correcting the false information all the climate change deniers put out. We get into demos sometimes, or even protests, but we're more of a behind-the-scenes sort of outfit. Like I said, we work with data."

"So tell me about climate art. Like what it is." *There's that smile again,* she thought. *That's going to get me into some trouble if I don't watch him*

He explained quickly about weather maps, weather statistics and weather trends being aggregated. Customers chose the data they wanted on his website then transformed it into three dimensional images. He explained that they compiled a database of all three, searchable by date, by location, by weather type. Then he talked about how it was output to a gismo to which he gave a name Tia didn't care to remember. He said it was a really clever algorithm that he had developed himself, based on an idea his Californian colleague had sent him

All he then had to do was convert the customer's data selection into a 3D-printable file that could simply be emailed anywhere in the world – anywhere with a high-fidelity 3D print shop that would take the commission. It eliminated any kind of delivery issues, so it saved on fuel consumption and on emissions. Finished pieces were three-dimensional and could be adapted into wall art or sculptures, jewellery or badges. Some people had designed trophies and drinking goblets and chess pieces using his data and his technology. Architects had even tried to take them on board and incorporate them into building projects, but there still seemed to be some limitations of scale that meant none of these had yet come to any sort of fruition. But his algorithm dealt with pretty much everything else

"Of course there's the birthday market too," he went on. "*Happy birthday, darling. Here's a statue of what the weather was like on the day you were born* or some such nonsense. The crap that people will buy."

There were also the people who wanted images in 2D - on a t-shirt or a greetings card something. Harry saw these as thoroughly unimaginative and a bit beneath him, so he charged a fortune for them. And still people bought them. He was about to launch into a description of some next-generation development – 4D printing that would allow the outputs to move or grow or breathe, as he called it - but Tia's head was starting to hurt so she reined him back in and returned to what had been stolen

"As you can see, the data is not all that sensitive," he told Tia, "just very useful to me. The algorithm that processes the data and produces the images might be worth stealing, but there's no way they can get their hands on that. So it just never felt worth securing the weather data, not even putting the discs in a drawer. I only keep it on CD because my computer is so old and could crash any day, otherwise it would all be on my hard drive."

Tia looked at Harry, noticed how deep and brown his eyes were, then asked, "So how does someone get into this weather art? What gave you the idea?"

Harrison's face lit up like someone who has been invited to hold forth on a favourite subject – which he just had been, as Tia would find out. "Even as a kid, when I looked at pictures, I always looked at the sky. When the artist hadn't bothered to draw something in – maybe I should say had chosen not to – I felt frustrated, cheated. I always wanted to see what the weather was like. Even in comics. Whoever used to draw Dennis the Menace or the Bash Street Kids hardly ever included weather – only as a plot device when they did, and never just as an ambient condition which is what it really is

"Then as I grew up, I started getting interested in art – art with a capital A. And what I got most excited about was the weather in the pictures I saw. Have you ever seen Constable's Salisbury Cathedral paintings? Turner's *Fighting Temeraire* is another one, or Hieronymus Bosch's *Gloomy Day*. There's really powerful weather in pictures like those. You can feel the rain. You can breathe the fog. But the daddy of them all, the one I became quite obsessed with for a very long time is *The Wave*."

Tia raised an eyebrow at this and queried, "The Wave?"

"*The Wave. The Hokusai Wave.* The blue and white Japanese wave. You've seen it on tea-towels or on mugs or … on all kinds of tasteless, trivial stuff."

Tia nodded – she thought she knew the one he meant

Harry was still enthusing. "I first saw it on a box of chocolates, I think. That's the one that finally made me aware of the way I feel about the weather."

"OK. I think I get it." Tia was beginning to realise what a driven man she was dealing with. "So that's two questions answered. That leaves one more - the police. Have you told them? And for when you tell me 'no,' as I'm sure you're going to, I'll save time and just add 'why not?' now."

Scowling ever so slightly, but holding her gaze, he said, "It's the activism, of course. I've got form with the cops. I've been arrested. Never charged, never been in court, but arrested more than once by more than one force. Certainly never done time. But I have had a couple of cautions and they do know who I am. All I ever do is exercise my democratic right to protest, and what ought to be my right not to get hit over the head. I'd rather just keep them out of it."

Not wholly convinced by his story, Tia nevertheless uttered a somewhat elongated *OK*, adding, "So you want me to investigate -

what? Who did it? Why they did it? What they've done with the booty?"

"Booty?"

"I used to read comics as well. And adventure stories."

Again, Tia and Harry exchanged smiles

The desk phone was picked up quickly when it rang. It was answered curtly. "DI Kowalski. How can I help you?"

"Hi John. It's T. You got a few minutes?" Tia Plenty and Detective Inspector John Kowalski were still nearly an item. Most of the time

"You know I've always got a few minutes for you, T. Just maybe not as many as there used to be."

"Look – that was not my fault, John. You know it wasn't." Tia Plenty could not believe she was still not forgiven. "I didn't know it was your last bottle of Blue. You normally have a year-round supply." Blue was a Belgian-style beer, locally brewed and only available in the run-up to Christmas. Detective Inspector John Kowalski seemed obsessed with the stuff. Tia liked it too, but within reason

"It still doesn't change the fact that you drank my last bottle without even asking. And there won't be any more till nearly Christmas."

"I'm trying for you. I am trying. There's bound to be some available. Somewhere. I am a detective, too, don't forget. I'll find some for you."

Tia couldn't see it of course, but Kowalski was grinning much in the style of a Cheshire Cat. Finally, he relented: finally, he decided he would let the lady off the hook she had so willingly if unwittingly attached herself to. But he was going to do it on his own terms. "But you drank my last bottle. You didn't ask. You just drank it. Just like that. Even the four kegs I've still got don't excuse that."

"You what?" Tia was really screaming down the phone

"So is that all you wanted in your few minutes, Tia darling? To apologise to me?" He really was enjoying this. "Because I have work to get on with."

"You really are enjoying this, aren't you?"

"Enjoying what?"

"I take it it's a quiet day for the SYPD?"

"There's no D in South Yorkshire Police. You know that."

"OK. Truce. I just want to run a name by you. See how you react."

"Investigator Plenty – I react by telling you I don't react at all to such questions. If I start giving you privileged information, they'll be after my warrant card. You know that too."

"I'll only be listening for the blank response or the sharp intake of breath. I'm sure it will be one or the other."

"You can read into it whatever you want when I don't say anything or react in any way. That's your choice. Just don't try to blame me for anything stupid you get into later."

"You're such a hero, John, such a fine, upstanding officer."

"Cut the flannel, T. Just tell me the name."

"Harrison Richardson."

The DI laughed – out loud. "Don't tell me he's getting his hooks into you."

"Thanks, DI Kowalski. I think that tells me what I need to know."

"Huh?"

"Don't worry about it, John. Enjoy your Blue. I think I'm going to be busy for a while."

Harry's phone buzzed. He was back in his flat. Then immediately it beeped. The day had been an unsettling one. As he was picking the device up, it made yet another noise, one that probably also began with a B: Harrison Richardson wasn't even going to dignify it with a name. Easiest app to open on his phone screen was Twitter. He found on his notifications a Tweet that read *How does it feel to have the #ArtRippedOut of you @WeWeathermen?* Facebook and email also had words waiting for him – much the same words. *How does it feel to have the art ripped out of you, hashtag.weathermen? How does it feel to have the art ripped out of you, Harrison Richardson?*

Harrison Richardson sank into serious thought. Who the hell was this? Whoever it was was good. Whoever it was knew a lot – more than could be accidental, more than was comfortable. Was this what it was like to be stalked? Would the PI come up with anything? He hadn't expected a PI to be a girl – a woman

After a couple of hours scouring the internet in her office, Tia thought she had pulled some meaty facts together. Hashtag.weathermen seemed to be just what Harry had claimed – an outfit dedicated to pointing out all the holes in the anti-climate change arguments. No hate mail or trolling in evidence, nobody with any real clout that she could see who was out to get them. It worried her slightly that they seemed to have named themselves after what was a fairly extreme left-wing activist group from the US in the 70s, but that lot had been quite ineffectual in the end and did little harm except to themselves. *"Just a bunch of poseurs it suited the authorities to appear to be scared of,"* she thought. Maybe this mob would be the same. *"Feed the rumour mill and keep most people in line. Nothing changes."* Before moving on to check out this so-called art, she had one last glance at his Twitter account and things had changed. *#ArtRippedOut* sounded quite aggressive, though it could still just be someone with a bizarre sense of humour

"You wanted to see me, sir?" The head that poked round Kowalski's office door belonged to DC Cunningham

"Yeah. Thanks, Cunningham – er, Keith. I need some information, well, advice really." Kowalski knew he was at the edge of his comfort zone, but he waved an instruction for Cunningham to come in and sit down. "And drop the *sir*, if you don't mind. Just for now. This is a bit, well, private – personal – man-to-man."

"Certainly sir," the DC responded, adding, a little too slowly, "John."

The corner of Kowalski's mouth smiled, without his consent. He tried to curb it. He failed. "I remember you had a run-in – no, I'll rephrase that. I remember you once came across an individual called Harrison Richardson."

"What's he done?"

"Nothing, as far as I know. It's what has been done to him. He's been burgled."

Grinning, Cunningham nevertheless said, "You won't be putting me on the case, will you sir? Familiarity with a suspect, sir, and all that."

"He's not a suspect, C… Keith. He's a victim. A possible victim. And I won't be putting anyone on the case because there is no case. Not yet. Nothing has been reported. All the same, I do have it on good authority."

"Is this from Tia, sir? I mean – Miss Plenty. John." Reversing two different modes of everyday address within a single conversation was proving a difficult trick for the young detective. "My turn to rephrase, I think." He drew in breath. "How much of what your source has revealed to you are you able to share with me? John."

"You're right. We can't keep this up can we, Cunningham? Let's just speak normally. But this remains an informal chat, yes?"

Relieved and finally relaxing on his chair, Cunningham said, "Sure thing, sir. What is it you want me to tell you?"

"Anything you can tell me about Harrison Richardson that doesn't pre-suppose he's someone we're after, no matter what either of us thinks."

Cunningham had much that he could tell Kowalski. And he did

Two men met on the stairs in a block of flats where they both lived. They often met on the stairs, it seemed

"Late start today?" the man climbing the stairs observed

"Late finish last night," the man descending replied. "Had to stay and talk to the boss. He was pumping me for details about a clown I've been after for a long time, so I was happy to help. Not a proper crim as such, but one of those smart-arse protester types. A bit of a tree-hugger. I'd love to see him banged up, if only for wasting everybody's time."

"You get plenty of those, I imagine."

"Enough. More than enough. Anyway – must go. See you next time."

"Ciao."

Sitting in front of TV. TV on but no sound – just some daytime home improvement garbage. Paid no it no mind. 'Fighting back was never part of the plan.' Single finger tapping on tablet. Slow, but encourages short messages. Hiring a PI when you had the #ArtRippedOut of you. Bad boy, @WeWeathermen. Calling cops, a bad move when you had the art ripped out of you, hashtag.weathermen *and* No one's gonna put it back now you've had the art ripped out of you, Harrison Richardson – we will be in touch. *Never thought he had the balls. 'Interesting'*

After a little more research, Tia realised Harrison Richardson was quite an easy man to keep tabs on. He was not exactly all over the internet, but his web presence was strong. His websites all ranked high, and his publications and merchandise were on every online selling site she could think of. He seemed especially well represented on her search engine's images tab, but then he would be. He had a look that made him stand out in his particular field of operation. He drew the camera. It was probably the suit that did it - the suits. He seemed to have an extensive wardrobe. "… and business suits are far from your classic climate-change protester outfit," she muttered. He used to have a beard too, a neat one that suited him well, but – no – she preferred him without, she decided. These were the thoughts that were occupying her when her phone sprang into life – *The Weather*

Girls. The track had been just sitting there on her phone doing nothing and she wanted a ringtone on his number that she would recognise instantly. It was what she always did with new clients who seemed like they might be important. *It's Raining Men - hallelujah* was the only weather track on there so it was a no-brainer

Why am I feeling so excited just because my phone is ringing? is what she thought when the tune kicked in. "Hi, Harry? It's T. Anything happening?" is what she said when she picked up

"I'll say it is. Have you reported me to the police?"

He sounded angry. "Reported you to …? No I haven't reported you to the police. I've …"

"Go on. You've what?"

"I asked one question of a contact of mine in the force. Just one." Client complaints usually concerned her doing too little for them, not too much. "I'm checking where the ground is. To lay down those ground rules, remember? Like I said when we were in the library."

"And like I said when we were in the library, I do not want the police anywhere near this. At all. There's nothing I do that's actually illegal, but there doesn't seem to be anything I can do to persuade the police. I'm sure there's a lot of coppers all just queueing up to put something over on me."

Sensing just a hint of over-reaction not far short of paranoia, Tia felt it necessary to try and reassure him. "It's not like on the old cop shows on TV, y'know. They don't have the time or the resources to invest in personal vendettas these days."

"So you say. But someone out there is trolling me. They know my name, they know about the burglary, they know about you and they know the police know."

"Is this the Art Ripped Out hashtag thing?"

"You've seen it, then?"

"It wasn't difficult, Harry. But I hardly think one Tweet, even one that has made itself sound quite aggressive, counts as trolling."

"It's not one Tweet, and it's not just Twitter. It's on Facebook, I've had emails. And it's not even only online. I have been burgled, don't forget. And how come whoever is doing it knows about you and about the coppers? I'll assume you haven't been blabbing to anybody but your policeman friend, so where else do we think the information is coming from?"

"You think the information is coming from the police?" Tia asked. She certainly did not

"Don't you?"

"You seem to be inviting me to draw conclusions based on a lot of supposition here. And I thought you were a scientist and a seeker after truth."

After a pause, he said, "Fair point. Maybe we need to start showing each other a little more respect."

Tia then added, "Maybe we should meet up again and sort the ground rules out better."

Harry cleared his throat. "Ms Plenty?" he asked with mock formality, "would you care to join me for dinner this evening? Well – I say dinner, but I can probably only run to bar snacks. I have just been burgled, y'know."

The call ended in laughter, which neither would have expected when it started

DC Cunningham was sitting in a coffee shop in town when in walked someone he knew – his neighbour

"You mind if I …," the neighbour asked

"Be my guest." Cunningham was not exactly relaxing at the moment. He was getting more uptight by the minute

"You look like you're not having the nice day they tell you to have at the counter."

Cunningham expelled air dismissively through his lips. "Like I told you earlier, I've got the boss on my case about this climate protester clown. It's starting to get me down." He took another sip of coffee and went on, "But it's not like I actually know the bloke. I arrested him once at a demo. Struck me as a bit of a smart-arse, but then he's a protester so what can you expect? But it's the way he dresses. When I asked him why he dressed like that …"

"Like what?" the other man asked

"None of your jeans or combat trousers, not anything you might expect. He wears suits. Smart suits. Expensive. Anyway, I asked him why and he said *out of respect*."

"He said what?"

"*Out of respect* – for us, for the police. The cheeky sod. Said he didn't want to waste our time by blending in with the rest of the mob. Wanted to make it easy for us to remember him."

"Seems to have worked."

"I suppose so. But I'm going to make him sorry he bothered. I'll make him regret the day he tried to take the piss out of South Yorkshire Police."

"What do you think he meant though? Respect? Odd thing for a tree-hugger to say?"

"I don't suppose he meant anything by it. Just trying to wind us up. Well two can play at that game."

"Sorry. It has not been possible to connect your call. Please try later."

Kowalski thought this was odd. Tia never turned her phones off. *Could be a dead battery*, he supposed. He tried again, this time on the business line

Another mechanical voice. "Sorry. It is not possible to connect you to …" "UrbanAgriTecs …" in Tia's voice. "Please leave a message after the …" He hung up

He wanted to apologise. He knew he'd been a bit of an arse earlier. He wanted to apologise and be forgiven. What had she told him? *Enjoy your Blue. I think I'm going to be busy for a while.* What did that mean? Was she punishing him? Or had he really blown it this time? Or – was she really just busy? Busy with Mr Harrison-*I-care-so-much-more-about-the-planet-than-you*-Richardson, no doubt. Tia was too smart to fall for all that hippy schmooze. Wasn't she? He sent her a text message asking her to call, then rang the pub and asked them to keep him some steak pie with chips. "No peas, though, please. I can't be bothered chasing those little buggers round the plate." There was football on the box later, and he might as well watch it on his own in there as watch it on his own at home

Front door locked. 'Not like last time. He's learned something.' Kitchen window – closed, locked. No matter. Not what he was here for. Not this time. Neatly folded sheet of paper taken from pocket – unfolded. Double-sided tape from different pocket. Fix paper to kitchen window. Walk away. Grinning. 'See what you make of that, you smug Brit.'

Dinner, such as it was, went well. The friendly, positive business relationship they had established earlier in the day was easily restored, along with a growing degree of personal warmth. Tia explained exactly what she had and had not revealed to Kowalski, also noting that the name seemed to mean nothing to Harry: John was one up on him there. She encouraged Harry also to think in terms of grudges – whether there was anyone out there who might consider they had some legitimate reason to want to take him down. All the while, she enjoyed the brie and bacon salad her client had bought for her. He kept up his onslaught on the pie he had bought for himself. With chips. No vegetables. When she expressed surprise that he wasn't a five-a-day man, Harry simply shrugged and took another forkful, and smiled at her with his eyes

Through his food, he told her, "I hope I am upsetting people – some of those selfish business bastards and corrupt politicians who still try to insist climate change is a conspiracy. If we're not doing that, then hashtag.weathermen is just wasting its time. But give you a name, a person or a business that might want to put the frighteners on me? On me personally? I can't do that. Nothing like this has ever happened to me before."

"Let me look at them again."

Harry passed his tablet across the table to Tia, saying, "The icons are all there on the one screen – Twitter, Facebook and Gmail."

"And you're sure I'm not going to find anything on here you wouldn't want me to find?" Harry responded by taking another forkful of pie and making fake talking-with-mouth-full noises. Tia flicked through the messages – there were still only six – then said, "And you've searched these names and handles and email addresses to see if that tells you anything?"

"Almost like it really is just some kid somewhere. But I'm not buying that. This is something a lot more ..."

"Scary?" Tia suggested

"I was trying to say professional, accomplished, organised – something like that. But I don't mind saying it scares me a bit. If someone is after you and you don't know who they are, you're going to be a bit scared."

"It's how he comes to know about the police that bothers me. Does he have a mole or just a good hack?"

This thought seemed to bring the conversation to a halt for the present. After a brief pause in which he polished off the last of his pie, Harrison leaned just a little closer to Tia and asked if she would like another coffee. Tia's plate had been empty for some time and now she drained the Americano she had been nursing. Looking straight back at Harrison, straight into his blue eyes, she said, "No. It looks like I could be busy from tomorrow, so I need a good night's sleep tonight. Another coffee and I shall be climbing the walls till morning."

Then he turned on the smile again. "I don't suppose there's any chance you would like to come and ... investigate the crime scene with me tonight."

"Why Mr Richardson." Tia always did good mock-indignation. "Just what kind of a private investigator do you think I am? What I do think is that you need sleep as much as I. We're going to have to get very busy in the morning if we are going to find this character."

Tia drove home and entered her terraced house through the front door, which was on the side of the building, in the passage. No mail was waiting for her on the mat. She went to the fridge and poured a glass of milk. A quick glance at her tablet showed no waiting emails. Turning on her phones, she found a missed call on each, both from Kowalski. The business phone showed there were also text messages, so she clicked through. The first one said he was sorry, that he wanted them to be friends again, or whatever they were. *Oh you old-fashioned romantic, John*, she thought. The next said he had information about the tree-hugger that she would want. It asked that she ring as soon as she got the message – if it was before midnight. Her phone said 10.47 which meant she had time to grab some chocolate to go with the milk, and time to reflect for a few moments on the startling differences – and the major similarities – between the copper and the tree-hugger, as they had mutually dismissed each other without ever having met

Both were men of strong conviction: despite only meeting him hours earlier, she knew this of Harry, and she knew John of old. Both knew what they knew and, because it was what they knew, they knew it was therefore right. Both men liked to take the lead. Kowalski was a DI, which he would not be if he couldn't lead. Harry had already tried hard to direct her actions – several times. He was the paying client, sure, but she was the expert in investigation, which had to count for something. More comically, both were unreconstructed men's men of a 70s/early 80s vintage. New Men they most certainly were not. *Whatever happened to New Men?* Tia wondered. And both liked to eat crap, heavy, stodgy crap with a crust, in prodigious quantities

Both were well-turned out, smartly dressed men – but that similarity ended very quickly. John dressed the way he did because there was a rule, a dress code, which said he should. As soon as he could get out of the suit, he got out of the suit. Harrison dressed the way he did because it was against the rules – the rules of his tribe, or so she was guessing. Most of his days he would spend amongst people for whom even jeans and a t-shirt seemed like the height of formality. Grunge, Goth, circus act – Tia did not know what this style might be called, but she knew she would recognise it whenever she saw it. And she was very sure Harry would have rejected it long ago. Dressing in a suit would be his rebellion even against the people he identified with most: even they were not going to push Harrison Richardson around

Suddenly, at the end of her chocolate bar, she remembered the task in hand and phoned Kowalski. His curt *where have you been?* did not sound like a man looking for forgiveness. And his *I can guess which one* response to her *out with a client* reply put the lid firmly on that idea. "Come on, Kowalski. It's late and I want to get to bed – alone. I've a busy day tomorrow, and I've a question for you if you leave me time to ask it. What have you got for me?"

"It's something he said in a statement when we arrested him round about a year ago. We asked him why he dresses the way he does and he said words to the effect of *out of respect for the police*. Said he wanted to make it easy for us to remember him. Sounds to me like he wants to provoke us. What do you make of it?"

"What do I ...? I think it makes him an arrogant man. Some men are arrogant, y'know. I think it probably makes him an effective protester too. Protesting is hardly a good career choice for a shrinking violet. There's no point doing it if you don't get noticed. And suits still get more respect in this world than jeans and t-shirts, so it sounds like a really good move to me."

"Well I'd like to haul his arse off the street," Kowalski almost growled

"And do what? Did you press any charges when you arrested him before?"

"No. There was nothing ..."

"You said it, John. There was nothing. Protesting is not of itself a crime. Shouting for something to be stopped or be started, to be banned or be introduced, is not a crime. And doing it in a smart suit may piss you guys off but it is not a crime and it should not be a crime. Now – can I ask you my question?"

"Like I said earlier, investigator Plenty, I cannot give you confidential police information. Doing that is a criminal offence, as it should be and as you should know."

"OK, detective inspector. Here comes my question. Who've you told about my investigation? Who knows about it apart from you and me, and my client?"

"Oh. T." His voice was relaxing a little. "I haven't told anyone. Of course I haven't. I'm a bit disappointed you even have to ask. Well -"

"Well?"

37

"Well, apart from Cunningham."

"That spotty youth you work with sometimes?"

"He's not that spotty. He's a promising young DC, and your boyfriend was his collar. I had to ask him what he knew. He naturally assumed we were lining Richardson up for another arrest, so I put him right. Told him we were talking about an alleged victim not an alleged villain."

"And now there is someone Harry and I believe to be his burglar taunting him online for having spoken to the police. Which he hasn't done. What does that tell you, John?"

Harry got out of his taxi and noticed it was wet underfoot. It must have rained whilst he was having dinner with Tia. He used the communal entrance to the block, not the front door to his flat. Everyone else used the place as a doormat, so he might as well. Inside the flat, he flicked on the corridor light and headed straight for the kitchen where he put the kettle on, then went to switch on the radio – but stopped when he saw something stuck to the window. To the outside of the window. A big sheet of paper with a message of some kind written on it. His windows were in need of cleaning so it wasn't easy to read, and the rain hadn't helped, but he made it out – slowly. It read:

you don't need a weatherman to know which way the wind blows

if you want your stuff back, call this number and do as it tells you

There was a mobile number and then a symbol, a logo

Harry recognised the logo – a crude line drawing of a rainbow and a flash of lightning. The Weather Underground, also known as The Weathermen

Underneath that, it read

don't mess with the weather underground

The words were cunningly all rendered in lower case, very 1960s as the artist in him knew, and no doubt done to blur the possible readings of the last line. He remembered where the top line came from – *You don't need a weatherman to know which way the wind blows*. It was Bob Dylan – *Like a Rolling Stone*, no – not that one. *Subterranean Homesick Blues*. That was it

The old Weathermen had taken their name from the song, and he had taken it from them. And if they were still around, or even if someone was just pretending to be them, it could spell serious bad news. They had been a pretty nasty direct action radical left-wing group back in late 60s and 70s America, back in the days of student activism and anti-war activism and civil rights activism and women's rights activism. It must have felt like you weren't anyone if you didn't have your own brand of activism in those days. He had been very young, only a kid, but he remembered seeing things on the BBC news. They had screwed up a Democratic convention. In Chicago maybe? He couldn't remember. They had blown things up, for real. They had threatened to kill people. He didn't think they had ever succeeded, but wasn't sure. *Was this really The Weather Underground?* he asked himself. *Did they still exist? Had they got back together again? Were they after him?* He called the number

After two rings, the call was answered – automatically, he could tell. A metallic voice, female, said, "Thank you ..." After a wholly unnatural pause, a human male voice, possibly American, said, "… Harrison Richardson …" pronouncing his name as two wholly separate unconnecting words. Then the metallic voice cut in again. "… for calling The Weather Underground." The male voice came back again at this point and sounded quite cocky, like it was trying to be provocative. "You know what we have. You know what we could do with it. If you want it back, go to Potus Lane, it's a short walk from your home, at 9.30 am tomorrow. There, you will see a sign. If you do not want it back, stay away and suffer the consequences." The message ended. Moments later, he re-dialled. He got exactly the same message. This was real. This was not a dream. Someone calling himself or themselves The Weather Underground was after him. Or herself, he finally acknowledged. This could be some old girlfriend, some disappointed ex-lover, bent on revenge, on payback of some kind. It could be any of many business people he had targeted with the hashtag campaign. It could be almost anybody

He needed to tell Tia. This, if anything was, was a job for his PI. But it was late. He sent a text message:

TIA: if you are awake, please call me. Something happened. Sthg big. Need to talk tonight or AM early – before 7. Call me. Harry

Turning back to the mug of tea he had started to make, he found it was almost cold, so he whipped out the tea bag and pushed the mug into the microwave to reheat, almost burning his fingers on the side of the mug as he took it out again, almost burning his lips on the rim of the mug as he tried to drink it, almost despairing as he waited for his phone to ring. The phone did not ring

He waited long enough, then went and set up his sofa bed, to sleep he hoped, though he worried his thoughts might not let him. He need not have worried. In what seemed like no time, his phone was ringing in his ear. It lived overnight on charge, easily reached from his bed. He had been too slow and sleepy to get to it before it rang off, but he picked it up anyway and would have looked to see who had been calling had it not rung again. He slid the green icon and grunted

"I was going to say *you are awake then*, but I think I'd better check first. Are you awake?"

He had managed to recognise Tia's voice and said, "Yes I'm awake. What time is it?"

"It's when you said – before seven. It's quarter past six if you want to get picky about it." Whilst Harry mumbled something about *middle of the bloody night*, Tia went on. "Your message said something had happened – something big. Do you want to fill me in?"

"Tia. Can I call you back in about ten minutes, when I've had a shower and got a cup of tea inside me?"

Half past six in the morning was not the sort of time Kowalski enjoyed arriving at work, but Cunningham had been quite excited when he phoned to ask for the meeting. Not excited – agitated. He had sounded agitated. He was convinced that today, they would really get the goods on *the hippy in the suit*, as he had taken to calling Richardson. He had had an anonymous tip-off telling him where Richardson could be found in a situation that would send him down for quite some time. All they had to do was turn up and take the necessary action

Promising copper though he was, Cunningham had shown signs of personal involvement, of harbouring a grudge, in matters relating to Richardson. Kowalski knew there had been far too much bad press for the police in recent years, especially for his force and, whilst this was not a high-profile case like some, it had the just kind of potential that could make it one if some undotted *i* or uncrossed *t* brought it all crashing down. He wanted to see Richardson stopped in his tracks as much as Cunningham did, but it had to be done by the book. He was thinking about Tia as much as anything

Harry next looked at his phone at twenty to seven. He had told Tia ten minutes, but taken twenty, maybe twenty-five. She would be getting impatient. He pointed his phone at the window, clicked and inspected the image. Then deleted it immediately. You couldn't read a thing. He tried again. This one was better. He sent the picture as an SMS to Tia, then rang her

"Long ten minutes, Harry," she said before he could say anything, and went on, "So tell me what this big thing was that happened last night?"

He explained – about the sign stuck to his window, about The Weather Underground, a leftie activist group he called them but admitted that these days they would be called terrorists. "Quite unfairly," he added

"And these are the people you named yourselves after?" Tia still felt shocked at this thought

He mumbled something about people taking things too seriously. "If I told you I'd named us after Michael Fish and Tomasz Schafernaker, how would you view that? A hurricane denier and a male model who does celebrity portraits on the side – they're weathermen too. And I bet you're too young to remember Wincey

41

Willis. Anyway, have you seen the picture I sent you? That will at least show you I'm not making this up."

"No, and I'll have to ring off to do it. I'll ring back in a couple of minutes. That's a couple as in two minutes."

Harry looked at his breakfast toast. He really wasn't interested. He knew he wasn't when he was making it. He did take a long draught from his mug of tea and, in the time that took, Tia was calling him back

"Fair enough. I've seen it. I'll buy it. Should I meet you at this – Potus Lane? Or shall I pick you up outside your flats?"

"You mean you think we should go and meet this person? Suppose it's a trap or something?"

"What do you mean *a trap*? You're back in those old TV cop shows again, aren't you? This is our only lead on whoever it is who burgled your flat and is sending you messages that are at least weird if not worse. We have to go there. There'll be two of us, so we'll be OK."

"But you're …"

"I hope you're not going to say I'm just a girl or anything."

It took him only a second or two to realise that *of course not* was the only acceptable answer. "Of course not."

Less than impressed, "I'll collect you," she told him

Turning into Potus Lane, it was immediately apparent where they should park – next to the near life-size statue of a Robin Hood-type figure that so obviously did not belong in the place where it stood. Harry was about to get out, but Tia stayed his hand. "Did you notice a red Audi parked up just before where we turned into this road? Two men in it."

"Can't say I did."

"Well they're policemen - Detective Inspector Kowalski, he's the contact I have mentioned to you, and if I'm not mistaken it's Detective

Constable Cunningham with him. And before you ask, no I haven't told them to be here. They obviously have their own sources on this one. But they are here, so they do seem to be taking it seriously because that is some expensive manpower on the case."

"Since we're passing on information, I suppose I could tell you that this statue – this monstrosity – is something someone has produced using my kit. It has to be one of the most ghastly examples I've seen, but I'm not responsible for the lack of taste of my clients."

"I'm very glad to hear that. I suppose we'd better go take a look at it because it must be the sign we've been promised."

An envelope was hanging from Robin Hood's arrow. Harry took it, ripped it open and read out its contents. "Good morning, Harrison Richardson. You are not #Weathermen. Drive down the lane, about 750 yards. Look left. Your next instructions are in the old barn." And that rainbow and lightning logo was there again at the bottom

Tia and Harry looked at each other. At least one shrugged. They climbed back in the car and set off, driving slowly and keeping an eye on the hedge that lined the left-hand side of the road. Soon enough, through a gap, they saw an old barn. Stuck in the middle of a field. After Tia found a place they could leave her car off the narrow road, they got out and walked back to the gap in the hedge. Spotting a familiar red Audi rolling down the hill towards them, Tia said, "We won't be alone for this one."

It took them just a couple of minutes to walk across the field to the barn. They peered inside, and it seemed empty save a load of anything-but-surprising agricultural detritus – plastic bags, random planks and other pieces of wood, a couple of non-matching metal wheel rims, a pitchfork that looked straight out of Thomas Hardy and other stuff. And of course, straw. When was an old barn ever devoid of straw? This one had a huge pile of the stuff that did not look entirely fresh. No human presence was apparent

"Hello?" Harry called out. His voice sounded hollow, and it went unanswered

He was about to repeat the call when a voice from behind him shouted, "Richardson. I want a word with you."

Harry and Tia both turned to see the figure of DC Cunningham almost silhouetted against the sunlight streaming in through the doorway. Tia also noticed Kowalski still a good distance away, walking across the field in his regular stately fashion. The young DC must have run across to catch them so soon, but he showed no shortness of breath

The policeman went on, "I have reason to believe that you, Mr Harrison Richardson, are carrying a package containing restricted substances which it is a criminal to possess. I would like to conduct a search of your person. Can I have your permission to do so?"

"What reason?" Harry demanded

"Somebody's snitched on you, so don't try and be clever. Just go and stand facing the wall and put your hands above your head."

"You're going to frisk me?"

Tia stood a little closer to Harry. "Shouldn't you be accompanied by a colleague when you carry out a search of this nature, Cunningham? For your own protection?"

"I am sorry you have to witness this, Tia – Miss Plenty, but this is a very serious matter and I have my duty to perform. And DI Kowalski will be here in a moment. He should be colleague enough for anyone."

Almost on cue, Kowalski walked into the barn. "Care to fill me in on what's happening here, Cunningham?"

"I'm just about to search Mr Richardson, sir. As you know we have reason to believe he has restricted substances in his possession."

"Well, go ahead then, Cunningham. But when you find nothing, we're going to need plan B."

Cunningham looked at his boss disappointed

Kowalski urged him, "Get on with it. Then we can rule the possibility out." Turning to Harry, he said, "You don't mind being searched, do you, Mr Richardson? I believe it is highly unlikely that we will find what we have been told we will find, but a tip-off is a tip-off and if it turned out you were carrying, I should be in very serious trouble. Miss Plenty will confirm that."

Tia nodded. Harry turned. Cunningham frisked. Nothing was found

All four then gathered together and Cunningham asked, "How did you know, sir? How did you know I wouldn't find anything?"

"Evidence, Cunningham. Evidence. Anybody can sling accusations around without any substantiation, but I looked on the internet. I have found enough evidence there to suspect someone is out to blacken Mr Richardson's name. He may get involved in things you and I would never approve of, but if there was evidence of a crime, we would have banged him up already."

From the loft in the barn, a voice suddenly rang out, sounding more than a little desperate. "Useless fuzz! Incompetent, useless fuzz! What do you think this is?" After a scuffling sound, a figure appeared at the front of the loft. "What do you think this is, you jerks?" The figure threw something down towards them. Cunningham picked it up carefully at its corner - a small polythene bag containing white powder. He showed it to Kowalski who told him to place it carefully and securely in his pocket

"I hope you don't think that's anything to do with me," Harry insisted

"Don't worry, Mr Richardson. We know it wasn't in your possession, so unless we find fingerprints or DNA to link you to it, you're in the clear."

Attention then returned to the man in the loft. Cunningham now realised he knew the man. "You're that bloke who lives in my flats."

"Congratulations, Detective Constable Cunningham. You finally worked it out. Can I thank you for having been such a good source of information for me? I have built this whole plan around the information you have shared with me all those times we met on the stairs."

Cunningham looked confused. Kowalski scowled at him, with sinking thoughts of data security breach in his mind

Harry turned to Tia. "Told you I couldn't trust the cops. Which one of these is your contact? Not the young one?"

Kowalski butted in. "No PI Plenty's special relationship is with me, isn't it Tia?"

Tia, ignoring Kowalski, instead called up to the man in the loft and asked, "Why? What's in this for you? What have you got against Harry?"

With a venomous look on his face, he answered, "He is not Weathermen. I am Weathermen. I am the last of The Weather Underground, keeping my father's memory alive. My dad gave his life for The Weathermen. There was an explosion in a Greenwich Village safe house, 1970. The dynamite they were making liberation devices with let them down. Blew them up."

"Liberation devices?" Tia queried. "You mean bombs. Bombs that would have been used to kill innocent people."

"Liberation devices. Bombs. Lollipops and rainbows. Who cares what you call them? But my dad died. Then this jerk, Mr Harrison goddam Richardson comes along and calls himself Weathermen. He's not Weathermen. My dad would want nothing to do with a buffoon like Harrison Richardson …"

Before the conversation could go further, the figure started backing away and they saw Cunningham make a sudden dash for the ladder leading to the loft. "He's going to get away!" he shouted

Rapidly Harry was following him. Reluctantly Kowalski did so too. Tia stayed on the ground floor, reasoning there was little she could do in such a melee in so confined a space. She hadn't reckoned with the weight factor though, but soon she saw the flimsy loft floor start to bow. She heard it start to creak. Dust was falling down. And wisps of straw. And suddenly, it gave way. Four heavy male bodies came crashing through, coming to rest on the pile of less than fresh straw below

Tia ambled across and stared down at the shocked and dishevelled forms. Grinning broadly down, she said, "Well what do you know? It's raining men – hallelujah." Then she added, "Is one of you professionals going to nick this guy?"

Kowalski and Cunningham, with their arrest, were heading back to the station to fill in all the paperwork and put their guest out of the way, for a while at least. Tia and Harry, both of whom would be required to make statements, followed in her car

"You did warn me it would be complicated," Tia observed, "and you weren't wrong."

"I'm sorry for what I seem to have done to that guy," Harry said. "He is not the kind we're trying to get at."

"He needs to be off the street though, if only for a while." Tia took a quick sideways glance at Harry, but he was staring straight ahead

"If you say so, Ms Plenty."

Noting the sudden formality, she went on, "There's just one thing I don't understand, Harry - the road name. Why do they call it Potus Lane?"

"It's not what you think," he replied, still staring absolutely straight ahead. "It's not what you think at all. It's Latin - potus - means a drinking vessel. Probably means there used to be a horse trough on the lane. Something like that. Nothing to do with Presidents of the United States. No conspiracy theories there."

"Are you OK, Harry? You seem a little ..."

"I seem a little what? Scared? Pissed off? I am. I need to take stock of what has happened. I need to separate myself from it - completely."

Not a little disappointed, not a little dismayed at this turn of events, Tia told him, reluctantly, "I'll get my invoice to you by the end of the week."

Kowalski's phone made the trilling sound that heralded the arrival of a text message. He punched it up. *Need to see you fast, John. Got important piece of evidence. Case of Blue. Tracked it down in a little shop I know. Evidence that I do care. On my way. T*

The Dragonfly

Susan Allott

The water trickled over the stones on the river bed, cascading over the large ones like mini waterfalls. I looked up into the sky where the radiant sun shone in all her glory sending rays of light into the nearby glades, so green, so lush, so rich in feelings. The gentle breeze threaded its way through the leaves and branches of the silver birch trees on the edges of the river. The sound was exciting, almost as if a conference of invisible creatures discussed the next move of nature.

"So, what will happen now?"

"I don't know," came the reply.

"I know," whispered another, "the birds will sing their early evening anthem."

Another whispered, "And then, as dusk descends, the sun will shed her crowning glory of red, yellow and orange hues as she lowers herself down into the land below."

"Yes, yes," breathed yet another voice. "The river will join in and bring to a crescendo her babbling notes and the slow bleat of sheep in acknowledgement of their appreciation. But not yet, there is still some time to go before this occurs."

The breathing tailed off, the breeze dropped, the leaves and branches stilled. Two rabbits played and jumped around just within my reach then, suddenly, ran off into the glade. I walked a little further down the path towards the weir which had an abundance of water cascading into the pond below. Something bobbed up and down on the water looking remarkably like a red ribbon near the offside bank, probably dropped by a cheeky magpie; they love bright pretty things.

The light sparkled like sequins on the water, it was like looking at a bale of glistening material flowing in the sun. The buttercups and celandines serenaded the banks in their floral patches of colour, yellow and white and oh the smell, yes, I do detect garlic flowers. They so enhance salads, I had already picked some of the leaves out of my garden and used them the week before.

Bluebells were coming out, the carpet of blue beginning to surround the trees, which were starting to wave as the breeze moved the leaves once again. Bees were taking into their pouches all the pollen they could find, I bet the honey will be good. I wonder how far they have come and when they get back, which direction they will perform their "waggle dance" to indicate to the other bees the direction of the flowers waiting to be pollinated. How I would love to be a spectator of the crowd to that information.

I looked at my watch, the glorious light in the sky was calming now, soon to be lowering her rays. The sandy bed was visible along with water lilies placed by some of the locals to encourage wildlife.

Suddenly, out of the corner of my eye, I caught something blue; gosh yes, it was a dragonfly. As blue as cobalt blue can be. She flew gently and smoothly over the top of the water, dipping and diving then landed on a lily pad. Her almost transparent wings still moving, her body spreading itself as if saying,

"Oh, this is a lovely place to rest and the sun is just catching the lily pad, so I have the best of both worlds, late sun and water and maybe food if I stay here long enough."

I watched thinking of the journey she had taken to reach this stage of her life. Cooped up under the water, larvae crawling up the stems of plants, builds herself a cocoon, growing her wings. She then crawls painfully up the stems of water plants and when her wings became dry, her virgin flight when she graces the world with her colourful flight. And for a short while those who watched were entertained by a wonder of nature. I sighed, thinking what wonderful things I had experienced and seen today.

As beautifully as she descended, the dragonfly quickly ascended onwards towards her destination. She would not have a long life but for as long as it lasted, she would be one of nature's jewelled assets of the waters.

I reached the end of the path by the sandy bed and there nearly hidden in the grass at the side of the bank, I spotted a child's small pink shoe. I smiled again, children loved this area. Paddling was a favourite because the water was shallow. The steps reached up to the road where I was heading, a noisy scurrying made me turn my head to the shrubbery on my left and eyeballing me with questioning eyes stood a badger. I stood still, and we locked eyes, I smiled at him. Our paths had crossed before, what a great creature he was, still brown with youth he hadn't got his stripes yet.

"Ay ay sir," I whispered, "I'm on my way." I smiled again, the badger sniffed, hesitated and walked back into the bushes.

I walked towards my Grandma's house. "No big red fox here then," I thought to myself laughing as I opened the door.

"That you girl?" came a soft old voice.

"Yes Nan," I replied.

I loved coming here. All my childhood had been spent roaming around these natural moors and the cottage with the quarry above and the river below. I lived in the cottages at the top of the quarry, so not far to come. The back of Nan's cottage had its own streams flowing over the quarry wall on to the pathways beneath in the garden where the toilet was. Now that was a scary place where spiders and other creepy crawlies surrounded me as I headed for the toilet seat. I never sat down in case something was on it. I used to take a torch and look around the jamb before and after entering this ungracious building. It didn't even flush, we still had middens as they were called. I used to envisage being pushed by a large spider and falling down the hole! "Enough," I thought with a shudder.

"Well what's it been today?" crooned my Nan.

I reiterated my findings and she was listening intently. She knew all the creatures around and about. Naturally, some even had names, as she fed the birds and gave corned beef to the foxes, badgers, hedgehogs along with whatever entered her doorstep, such as Dixie the cat and Flossy the little terrier from up the row of cottages.

The light was going fast, so I offered to make tea for both of us.

"What's been happening here this week?" I asked. We had this sort of conversation every week, it was such a part of my life. Dixie came to the door, which was nearly always just off the sneck, followed by Flossy. I laughed, they were such a funny pair. Nan always had titbits for them. I fussed Dixie, Flossy not wanting to be left out jumped on to my knee. Putting her down, I washed my hands and got on with the tea.

"What are you going to poison me with this time?" Nan asked me laughingly.

"Corned beef plait with tomatoes and pickle," I replied slurping my tongue in mischief. I'd persuaded her to let me put some frozen pastry sleeves into the freezer, so I could do something quick for us.

"Sounds good to me."

The sound of marching footsteps could be heard approaching the door.

"Who do you think those marching shoes belong to?" I asked.

Before she could reply, the door swung open and Mrs G from the third cottage marched into the room.

"Well, what on earth's up with you Mrs G?" I questioned.

"You look like you're on a mission girl," said my Nan looking concerned. She called everyone 'girl', it was something she had grown up with. There were so many of them, her mother called all the female siblings 'girl'. Then she didn't get the names wrong if she forgot what they were called. Well there were 11 of them.

"I've just had the police at my house, Nellie. You'll never guess what, there's been a death in the pond." Folding her arms, she finished with an air of importance and nod of the head.

"No!" gushed Nan, "Who was it?" she said with bright eyes.

"Well it's that young woman at the top cottage, policeman says it were this afternoon, she'd drowned."

"Really. Jane weren't you near there this afternoon?" asked Nan.

I stopped filling pastry cases, feeling shocked, the corned beef neglected. I thought about my walk and stop at the weir, where the 'pond' is. Before I could reply there was a knock at the door which stopped the conversation.

Mrs G rushed to open the door and there stood Constable Jenner. She beamed at him, hopefully. Always a smile for the gentlemen had our Mrs G.

"'Scuse me ladies," he wheezed: he wasn't at his youngest. "Can I ask you some questions?"

"Of course you can young man," said Nan cheekily, eyeing him up. "What's going on?"

Mrs G frowned, clearly not approving of Nan. You see, we realised that our Mrs G was after a man. She had already been after Nan's lodger last year but, he upped and left to work for the Waterboard, or 'Watterbord' as locals called the dam house on the other side of the valley, close to the peaks.

Constable Jenner coughed and pulled out his notebook. Licking his pencil he replied, "Earlier this afternoon a body was found in the pond and she has been identified as Mrs Ellen Connor of the top house of these cottages. I wondered if you could highlight at all any movements or anything suspicious you could tell me about."

Mrs G folded her arms, fidgeted with her apron and beamed at our Constable.

"Well I've told you everything I know. There was a bit of a row this morning, I were putting milk bottles out, children were shouting and then all went quiet. I thought it were just one of those rows they sometimes had when it all went quiet.

"I didn't really take much notice 'til the meowing of Dixie, as if she were crying and had been kicked. That man's a waste of space, he's horrible to her an' kids."

Nan said she had not heard anything and had been in all morning except for the visitations of Dixie and Flossy.

"What about you miss?" said Constable Jenner, irritatingly licking his pencil again. Doesn't he know it's not good for him?

"Well I remember seeing a red ribbon floating on the far side of the pond. When I reached the sandy bed, I noticed a small child's pink shoe on a large pebble at the bank side, where I was watching a dragonfly. In fact, if I hadn't been, I probably wouldn't have noticed

53

it. A badger came out of the bushes and went back again. After that I came here. Do you think these things might have anything to do with this situation?" I asked him.

Constable Jenner looked seriously at the small puzzled group and gravely explained.

"You see, the children are missing, we can't even begin to wonder what has happened to them. Nothing was found in the pond."

He turned to Jane.

"Do you think we could take that walk along the footpath where you've been?

"Er yes, certainly, I'll just get my jacket. Sorry Nan, tea will have to wait." I kissed her head, smiled at the frowning Mrs G who obviously thought she was being left out and walked down the path to the river.

"Be careful dear," Nan called out.

We approached the sandy bed gingerly looking around and then I saw the pink shoe.

"It's here," I yelled. I passed the shoe to him and he promptly brought out a plastic bag from one of his many pockets, carefully placing it into the bag.

"Thanks," he said gratefully. "Now let's go to the pond."

We walked quickly along the path reaching the weir pond.

"Look there it is," I cried, pointing to the ribbon on the far side. "How on earth are we to retrieve that?

I thought if I could cross the weir at the narrow part of the river, I could just skirt round and reach the other side. This I imparted to Constable Jenner, he agreed saying to be careful.

I did just that and narrowly missed falling into the weir but managed to catch my footing on a stone ledge embedded into the bank. I climbed on to the grass bank looking at the red strip of ribbon, which by now had floated towards the edge. On the third try, I caught hold of it and headed back to the other side with the wet item in my pocket, not very forensically good but better than nothing.

I gave the ribbon to Constable Jenner, who placed it in another plastic bag and we walked back to the sandy bed. A rustle sounded from the bushes as we reached the steps. We turned to see the badger creeping through the undergrowth. He looked at me again, he knew me from the last and all the other times we had met, so he wasn't really bothered. Then his head turned to my colleague. His wary eyes locked on to Constable Jenner who gasped, he had never come this close to a badger before.

"Are we safe?" he whispered starting to shake.

"Of course, as long as you stay still. He's okay."

The badger moved backwards into the bush, came back and performed the same ritual. I suddenly realised that he actually wanted us to follow him. I know this sounds unusual, but I have always thought all animals have a bit of collie sense in them.

"I know this sounds daft, but I think the badger wants us to follow him."

"What? Are you having a laugh Jane? He tried to splutter quietly.

"Oh c'mon, let's go." I smothered a giggle and grabbed his arm, pulling at his sleeve. "C'mon."

We pushed on through the undergrowth. The badger kept on going, not looking back until he reached a small clearing about ten yards from the path then disappeared. It was a rough area. Constable Jenner stopped, put his arm out to stop me going any further, gulped then grabbed my arm.

"Look, look," he pointed towards a far tree, his hand shaking. "What do you make of that?"

I looked, gaping. There under the tree were the bodies of two children. We ran forward hoping with every step the worst hadn't happened. We stopped, looking down on the two little ones. Kneeling our first move was to check their pulses.

"I don't think there is one. Look at the girl's neck, there are marks around as if she has been strangled." The same applied to the little boy. We looked at one another, my eyes filled with tears. "What on earth has been going on with this family?" I sobbed.

A sound stopped me sniffling. It seemed to come from the boy. I watched as Constable Jenner gently lifted the small body on to his knee and tried the pulse again.

He looked at me, tears filling his eyes. "I can feel a beat Jane."

I tried the girl again, lifting her little body slowly onto my knee and supporting her head. Her mouth moved, as if to let her tongue through.

"She's alive," I gasped. "We have to call an ambulance. I'll run to my Nan's, she has a phone, I made sure of it last year."

I ran like the wind, flew into the cottage, trying to relate in between breaths to the two women. Dixie and Flossy even sat as if listening to what had happened. I dialled 999, requesting police and ambulance to the bridge.

I found out later that, Constable Jenner sat stroking the hair of the twins and talking to them as if his own. His gentle voice eventually getting through to the children, who responded by at least trying to open their eyes.

"Come on Annie don't let me lose you now. Come on Jimmy," he sobbed, "look at me please."

His hip flask did not have the water he wished for but wet his hankie with the whiskey contents and rubbed it on their lips. He knew the taste wouldn't be nice but at least he would get a response from them. He tried to keep the children warm by covering them with his jacket and rubbing their limbs gently to keep the blood flowing through their veins. His heart lifted when he heard the sirens.

The ambulance team carried the children in stretchers to the awaiting vehicle. "All hope is not lost," the driver assured Constable Jenner and me. More police arrived, and statements were taken from us both. Constable Jenner received a grateful handshake from a more senior ranked officer as did I, very happy to be included.

Back at the cottage, the two ladies had been watching the activities over the wall, then later they were given first hand, the story by a proud Constable Jenner.

Apparently, the husband had been drinking the night before and was still under the influence in the morning. He worked in the clay mines down the valley. It was hard work and he walked there and back, and of course, called into the local pub before coming home. He rarely gave Ellen money, as he had spent his wages, he also liked to gamble and thus it was that Ellen had bravely decided to let him know that she had had enough of this life. Her children were suffering, and she was leaving him.

Cyril didn't like this at all and became angry, threatening to kill them all. He then seemed to sober up and stop shouting, only to drag Ellen, who was of slight build, down the cutting between the gardens, crossing the road into the snicket leading to the pond. The children had seen this and followed. He pushed his wife into the water and turned on the children.

They ran towards the sandy bed, towards the bushes but not before he caught them and tried to strangle them with his belt. They passed out through shock and lack of oxygen, but it was not enough to kill them. Thinking they were dead, he dragged them into the clearing out of the way and then ran off.

Later that week, the headlines of the local newspaper delivered to the cottages, told the story of the capture of the elusive, violent husband Cyril Connor, who was charged for murdering his wife and the attempted murder of his two children. Later he was sentenced to life, he was never coming out again. The children were safe and so was everyone else.

"What a horrible situation that was and to think he only lived up the row. What's going to happen to the children Nan?" I asked. This time I brought tea with me to be on the safe side. The last tea ended up being corned beef sandwiches and not in a plait.

"They've gone to Ellen's sister and husband. She doesn't have any of her own, so she is adopting them. They're a nice pair and so lucky to have pulled through all this. They wouldn't be here if it weren't for you and Constable Jenner. Have you heard? They're giving him a medal. He might smile a bit more now. "

"That's good," I said and smiled. "What a week. I think I might have to try a different walk next week. There's too much pain around that area. It will change with the winter though and when spring arrives, a new scene will appear, new dragonflies, new birds and flowers. The badger is the hero though. Before I go home, I am going to try and find him and leave him a treat. He deserves it."

"Quite right," said Nan. "By the way, did I tell you that his name is Billy? He comes to the garden quite often. He loves corned beef." She finished with a knowing smile.

"What, well you crafty one," I said laughing, "I wondered why he was so tame. He frightened the pants off Constable Jenner at first. Took me all my strength not to laugh out loud when I saw his face, poor lamb.

"I don't think Mrs G stands a chance with him. She forgets his wife is what the French call 'formidabla' a rolling pin springs to mind."

We both cried with laughter, life could be filled with the more simple and peaceful things again, like the nature around us. Dixie had now taken up permanent residence with Nan, much to Mrs G's disgust. "Why has he chosen you, he came more to ours than yours," she would chunter.

We knew, Nan was more generous with the corned beef. This humble tinned food played into everyone's life around here. Flossy still visited, was much loved and fussed and life became all the richer again.

Danger at Ramsey Manor

Phil Warhurst

Both the children had spent the whole journey engrossed in their technology and had no idea where they were and how they had got there. Only now as the car drove up a wide tree lined road on a shallow incline did they look up to see the massive grey edifice in front of them and what a surprise they got. Neither had expected Great Aunt Ada's house to be so huge. And spectacular! The house and their short stay there suddenly grabbed all their attention.

"Are we really staying here?" exclaimed Lucy.

"Wow!" was all that Jack could manage as he stared up at the building. The car swept around the drive and stopped in front of the massive main door. The driver, who had been sent to fetch them, jumped out of the car and opened the door to let them out.

"If you would follow me please," he announced. "Someone will bring in your luggage later."

He walked up to the door with the two children trailing behind him, open mouthed and cowed. He pulled on a wire hanging high above the door and a bell which resonated like Big Ben rang inside the house. After a few moments they could hear bolts being pulled back on the inside and gradually the towering door creaked open. A very tall, elderly man in a black and grey suit peered around the door and looked the two youngsters up and down.

"Ah," he wheezed, "Master Jack and Miss Lucy, I believe. Welcome to Ramsey Manor. Please come this way." And with that he turned back into the entrance hall and started walking to a magnificent wooden staircase that spiralled up to the next floor. The children followed him silently as their eyes spun round trying to take in everything they could see around them. They slowly climbed the stairs and reached the first floor and turned left along the passageway. A few doors down the suited man stopped at one of the room doors.

"This is your room, Miss Lucy," he announced, "and the one across the corridor is yours Master Jack. Someone will bring up your luggage and then you should get ready for dinner. Please come down when you hear the gong ring at seven." And with that he turned and disappeared back down the stairs much quicker than he had come up them with the two youngsters following his every move with wide eyed astonishment.

"I feel like we have gone back in time to one of those old Sunday night programmes that mum and dad like to watch," laughed Jack. "I'll go and change my shirt and come to your room in ten minutes."

Just as Jack knocked at Lucy's door on his return the gong rang three times downstairs. Lucy came out already changed with a bright flowery dress on.

"Ok," she said, "shall we go down and brave it?" They walked down side by side such was the width of the staircase. When they reached the bottom the suited man from before was waiting to greet them.

"This way please," he said as he gestured towards a large dark brown wooden door which the children assumed must be the dining room. The man turned the knob, opened the door and then stood back to allow them to enter. "Miss Lucy and Master Jack!" he announced as they walked in.

It must have been about nine o'clock when the pair arrived back in Jack's bedroom and they both jumped to sit on the edge of the bed while giggling wildly.

"Well that wasn't so bad!" laughed Jack, "Great Aunt Ada is really sweet and kind despite being a bit old fashioned."

"Yes," said Lucy, "that's true. What about those other two people? They were a bit unusual!"

"They were," replied Jack, "that little round Frenchman with the huge moustache and the old lady who smiled and said little but fiddled with her handbag! Very weird!"

60

"I think the man was Belgian," contradicted Lucy, "but they were both very interesting. Bet they've got loads of stories to tell. You know what we should do after we've had breakfast tomorrow?"

"Explore the house!" they both shouted together.

It was half past nine the following morning when they started their trip of discovery around the house. They went down into the kitchens and bade good morning to Mrs Lewis, the cook, who was already starting to prepare lunch. They then climbed the back, winding stairs which led them up into the house. The first floor they came to had a long corridor covered in dark floral wallpaper and a swirly red carpet. The place had a feeling of grandeur. They went into the first room on the left and it turned out to be a very well stocked library. It had full book shelves all around the walls and one of those long ladders attached to rails above and below the books which Jack couldn't resist the temptation to ride on!

Lucy said, "Come on. We'll come back and have a look at the books another time. Let's go to the top." They went back to the staircase and climbed up as far as it would take them. At the top they came to a tiny landing with a small banister. Only one old dark wooden door led off the landing. Lucy looked at Jack and he gave a hardly perceptible little nod encouraging her to open the door, which she did. Inside was quite a large cavernous room with bare floor boards and no wallpaper. The only thing in the room was a large highly decorative wardrobe. Lucy walked over to it and carefully opened the door. Jack came up behind her and peered over her shoulder. Inside the only thing they could see was a few fur coats at the front. Lucy pushed these aside and realised the wardrobe went quite a way back, so she stepped inside and started to inch her way forward. Jack cautiously followed her. After a few moments they found themselves in the dark and suddenly Lucy gave out a loud exclamation,

"Oh!"

"What's the matter?" Jack whispered, quite fearful now.

"I've just bashed my nose on the back of the wardrobe!" She whined. "Nothing to see here let's get out!"

Having both got quite claustrophobic in the wardrobe they both felt they needed some fresh air, so they headed out to the garden. The sun was out, and it was quite warm, so they sauntered around smelling the roses and looking at the apples which they might scrump later in their stay. However, they suddenly saw a couple of dilapidated buildings at the bottom of the lawn and both whooped and ran down the garden with arms outstretched like an aeroplane. The first building they came to had obviously been a small stable with a couple of partitions showing where the horses would have been kept. Next to that was a squarish shaped stone structure with a very large door open at the front. This seemed to be an old garage. As soon as the stepped over the threshold they saw a dirty, dusty sheet which was obviously covering some sort of machine. Pulling back the side of the sheet they realised that it was a car. It was an old car but somehow it looked futuristic. It was flat at the front and quite streamlined. It used to have some sort of shiny metallic outer colour, but this was now all tarnished and rusty. Jack pulled the sheet back even further, so he could get around the back and then he bent down to read the make and model.

"D. E. L. O. R. E. A. N." he spelt out, "DeLorean! Not heard of that one." They tried to find a door to open to see inside but they didn't find any handles or doors for that matter. In his frustration Jack banged his hand against the side of the car.

"Stupid car!" he shouted but just as he had said that the whole side of the car swung up and revealed the inside. They both looked astonished for a moment but then they crawled into the two seats and started looking at the controls.

"Look" pointed Lucy, "there's a button here that says 'START'!"

"Push it then!" screamed Jack. And Lucy did! There was an almighty sound as the engine started, smoke filled the garage and the lights started flashing. And then all of a sudden, the engine spluttered and cut out, the smoke stopped billowing and the lights went out. The car was dead.

Later that day Lucy and Jack decided to go for a short walk and explore the nearby village. There was a footpath which ran through the western side of the estate and then through the graveyard of the village church, St. Justin's. This came out into the cobbled little square of the village which consisted of a quaint looking pub, a post office and a small village store. On the small green next to a duck pond stood what looked like an ancient pair of stocks. Lucy and Jack took it in turn putting themselves in the stocks and the other pretending to throw rotten tomatoes at them. They wandered into the store and had a little explore before eventually buying some bars of chocolate and boiled sweets and then they sat down on a bench on the green overlooking the pond and facing into the lovely sunshine. They both thought all was well with the world and that coming to stay at Ramsey Manor and the village of Ramsey had been a great piece of good fortune. As they sat back in the sun Jack suddenly exclaimed,

"What's that over there?" He was pointing across the other side of the green, slightly to the side of The Quiet Woman, where there seemed to be a large box about ten feet high with some sign on the top which they couldn't read because it was facing the other way. They walked across the green to take a closer look. When they got around the other side they could read that the sign said "Police". There seemed to be a door in the other side and now they could see small windows at the top.

"I've seen these before in history books," said Lucy, "they are police boxes. Not quite sure what they are for though." Jack looked intrigued and went up to the door and put his hand on the handle.

"I'm not sure you should do that, Jack," said Lucy, "it does belong to the police after all!"

Undeterred Jack turned the handle and pushed on the door. It creaked open and Jack turned to Lucy and smiled mischievously.

"Don't!" implored Lucy, but Jack ignored her and stepped into the box.

"Wow!" he shouted in excitement, "you'll never believe what's in here Lucy!" Despite her misgivings Lucy crept into the box behind Jack. She gazed around the box and saw immediately what Jack had been amazed by. On every wall in every space were pictures of naked women, some torn out of newspapers, some in calendars and some small photographs.

"Quick Jack. Get out!" Lucy screamed and then got hold of Jack's shoulders and pushed him outside. "That's disgusting!" she snorted, "how do they manage to get away with that! Jack you must forget what you've just seen." Jack didn't show much reaction. He just continued staring into space all the way back to the house.

That evening Jack and Lucy decided to go down early for dinner. They wandered down to the library to take a look at the books. As they walked in they were aware of a strange sound coming from one corner of the room. It was a clickety-clack sort of noise. When they looked over to the far corner they saw a large leather winged chair and sitting quietly in the corner knitting was the little old lady from last night. She stopped knitting and looked over to see who had just come into the room.

"Hello dears," she said almost in a whisper, "have you had a good day?"

"Yes thank you," replied Lucy, "we explored the house and the village."

"Anything interesting?" asked the old woman. Lucy and Jack looked at one another and both shrugged at said at the same time,

"No not really."

"Do you mean there was nothing interesting about the wardrobe or the car or the police box?" Lucy and Jack both stood with their mouths wide open.

"How did you know about those things?" asked Jack.

"When you get to my age you know most things," she replied enigmatically.

"Have you been following us?" ask Lucy.

"No," she replied.

"Then how could you possibly know, Miss... sorry I've forgotten your name," said Lucy.

"It's Miss M…," and just at that moment the dinner gong went drowning out what the lady was saying. She then got up and said, "we need to go into dinner now."

They had a lovely meal of roast beef with Yorkshire puddings and then the apple pie was brought in. Jack was just about to tuck into his when the little round man with the extraordinary moustache gave the slightest of coughs, stopping Jack in his tracks.

"Excuse me young man but I wouldn't eat that if I were you. It may be very damaging to your health." Everyone around the table suddenly stopped eating and looked across to where Jack had frozen in the process of putting his spoon into the bowl.

"Whatever is the problem?" asked Great Aunt Ada. The little man, who they knew was French, or possibly Belgian, looked around the table and realised that he had everyone's attention.

"The problem is Madame," began the man, "that I, the greatest detective in the world, have noticed that this is the tastiest Tarte de pomme that I have ever tasted and that if I don't get a second helping I will have to show my frustration in some ghastly way and seeing as Master Jack seems to have the biggest piece I would rather it was his!" At this the tension was broken and the room exploded into laughter above which Aunt Ada shouted,

"There is no problem Monsieur. We have some more downstairs that we can get you. Young Jack will not need to be viciously robbed of his portion."

As they walked up the stairs to bed that evening Jack turned to Lucy on the top step and said,

"Are you enjoying yourself?"

"Yes, in a way," replied Lucy, "it's very lovely here and the people are definitely interesting, but I thought something a little more dramatic might happen."

"Yes, I know what you mean," said Jack, "perhaps we should take a break?"

"Right let's do that," said Lucy, "and we can come back another time?" They both walked past their rooms and came to the wall at the end of the corridor.

"End programme!" announced Jack and at that the corridor just phased away as did the rest of the house and the other people in it. Two young people now stood alone in a square room with a network of beams all around them. They walked forward and as they did so a panel in the wall slid back mechanically and allowed them to exit the room. They emerged into a corridor with flashing lights on the floor and ceiling.

"Did you write that programme?" asked the young woman who was now back to her normal height and age.

"Yes," replied the young man, also returned to his own strapping physique. "I think I know what I did wrong. I asked the computer to research twentieth century culture and discover any mysterious fantasies it could find. I think it got mixed up with the genres and chronology and gave everything a twenty third century explanation all full of reason and science without the mystery. I'll work on it tomorrow and see if I can make it more interesting."

Just at that a tall, athletic bald man in a slightly different uniform came around the corner. They both stood to one side and as he walked past he said to them,

"Goodnight Ensigns!"

"Goodnight Captain," they both replied together and then continued walking along the corridor.

The LWC and Damned by 'I do'

Sharon Brady-Smith

Our community had assuaged our consciences. We held a few marches, signed a petition and wrote strongly worded letters to MPs and newspapers. The more religious among us prayed to their God or Gods. When our efforts failed we shrugged our shoulders and said to each other, 'It's such a shame, but what more could we do?' We in the Ladies Who Can (LWC) did what we did best and held a bake sale and a raffle to raise funds to buy them a few luxuries, so they could spend their last few days on Earth in comfort and then went about our business.

I was the worst of them. When Fran suggested a further baking session, 'to donate to the poor unfortunates themselves,' I'd grumbled at the extra time and expense then baked the simplest recipe I knew (lemon drizzle cake) and driven over to Fran's house on the Saturday afternoon to drop it off.

She and Doreen waited for me, sitting in deck chairs in the sunshine on her drive. 'I'm so glad you brought your car Trudy. Could you just run everything over to the facility?'

'I'm busy,' I'd pleaded with Fran, 'can't someone else make the delivery?' I'd known it was pointless. Even as I argued with Fran, Doreen was loading the hatchback of my car with a dozen assorted plastic tubs.

'I don't drive dear,' she said patiently. 'Maureen has broken her ankle and Eveline is waiting for her cataract operation. There is nobody else.'

She thrust the letter with directions and instructions into my hand and I conceded with poor grace. It was the biggest drawback of being one of the younger members of the LWC. The senior members bossed me about something terrible and I hadn't the nerve to complain.

On the hour-long drive the fickle English summer weather deteriorated to match my mood. I decided, yet again, to stop volunteering. I had done my bit. I didn't enjoy being a volunteer and I didn't like people. Oh, I suppose I didn't mind donating an occasional cake, but I would stop being involved in the meetings. It wasn't as if I felt a part of their stupid community. That was why I'd joined the LWC in the first place and it had made no difference.

The facility had once been a secure Victorian mental hospital. It had closed in the Eighties and stood vacant ever since. The main building was Grade II listed, so developers couldn't simply knock it down and rebuild, but the various proposals for the site, including flats and a hotel, had always fallen through at the last minute. The slightly sinister building suited its current purpose well.

As I reached the main gate, the heavens opened, and torrential rain poured down. Two guards stood, huddled in the poor shelter of sentry boxes. I wound down my car window to speak to the closest and show him my documentation, but his fellow guard had peered inside the car. He shouted above the roof. 'It's another one stuffed with cakes.'

The guard on my side shook his head and waved me through. 'Stay on the main drive. There are parking spaces in front of the house.'

As I parked, another guard came to greet me. He wore a plastic poncho over his uniform and held an umbrella above the car door, protecting me from the elements as I climbed out.

'Afternoon Ma'am, we didn't expect you until 5:00 pm.'

'I'm sorry,' I reached back into the car for my letter and gave it another quick glance, 'I don't have a time on here. Do I need to come back?'

'Of course not. If you'd like to follow me Ma'am.' He held his arm out to the side, gesturing the direction I should follow.

I ducked from beneath the umbrella and opened the hatch to grab the first pile of containers. 'Are you allowed to give me a hand?'

He followed me to the rear of the car. 'What with?'

I dumped the first stack of containers in his arms. 'The cakes of course.'

He stared at the load in his arms and blinked a few times. 'You're donating cakes?'

'Yes, from Loxington LWC.'

He started to laugh so hard I thought he would drop his load. 'I'm sorry. I thought you were somebody else.'

'Didn't the guards at the gate say I was coming?'

'Yes, they did. I'll have words with those two jokers later, but there's no harm done.'

The guard helped me carry cakes along a windowless but wide wooden-panelled corridor with polished parquet floors. The clicks from my kitten heeled shoes echoed forever in the eerie silence.

We passed through an imposing arched door into a large dining room that must have been designed by a different architect: one who had an unrequited love affair with arches. After the oppressive corridors, the pseudo-gothic style windows bathed the room with natural light, bright even with the cloudy sky.

The room was devoid of life and colder than the simple lack of sunshine warranted. Modern plastic tables and chairs were at odds with the architecture and there were not enough of them to fill the room, so they clustered in a corner by the entrance as if afraid. One table stood alone, piled high with plastic cake containers.

'Oh dear. Do they not have a sweet tooth or, are they inundated?'

'I didn't know you could drown in cake,' he said. 'These poor buggers are but they're having a good go at eating them all.'

'There will be no cake where we are going,' said a bass voice from directly behind me.

I hadn't heard him coming down the corridor. I jumped and spun towards him, almost losing my load in the process. He obviously expected my response and caught the tubs, laughing as he did so.

69

'Earth breeds such timid little women. It is no wonder they only provide cake and not what we need.'

'I am Vonn. Which is your offering?'

I stood, gawping at the first 'live' alien I had ever met. If his vertically-slitted pupils had not alerted me to his predatory nature, his fangs as he laughed at me might have clued me in. There was far too much corpse-pale blue skin on display because he only wore cropped trousers, reminding me of a zombie Incredible Hulk. Even so it was the scars that held my attention. I'd never seen so many on a single person. Neither had I ever been so intimidated or repulsed by physical appearance. Vonn was the most horrific sight I'd ever encountered outside of a cinema.

I knew they were bigger than humans. However, knowing and seeing are entirely different. His hands were the size of dinner plates and he was barefoot. Probably because average shoeboxes wouldn't fit on his feet. Of course, there *were* humans this big, but they were the likes of 'Andre the Giant' or 'Lou Ferrigno' not the average bloke on the street. At least not around Loxington.

'They're gifts, not offerings,' I replied, relieved that my voice didn't squeak like the mouse he'd labelled me.

He stopped laughing and shrugged with a single shoulder. I found his regard unnerving, as if he judged me. Some of my sympathy evaporated on meeting Vonn. I didn't like him.

'Even so, which *gift* is yours?' he asked again.

I wasn't sure I wanted to tell him. 'I'm sorry you don't want them, I'll take them away.'

'I did not say we wouldn't accept your gifts, only that you don't bring what we need.'

'And what would that be, exactly?'

'A legal basis to remain.'

My guard-cum-guide had by now deposited his load on the table of *offerings* and relieved Vonn of his load of rescued baked goods. 'That's enough Vonn,' he said.

'And what exactly would that be?' I asked.

'Are you cruel, or do you not know the terms?'

'I'm warning you.' The guard stepped between Vonn and me. I thought him either brave or foolhardy, but as he produced a pen shaped object from his pocket, Vonn dropped his gaze to the floor and stepped back.

Something that big and scary shouldn't be afraid. I looked over to the table holding the cakes, found the one I'd baked and placed it in Vonn's hands. 'This one's mine. It's a lemon cake.'

'Would you deliver it to my brother's cell? Sidar might enjoy a visit.'

'Cell?'

'The suicidal are confined for their safety,' said the guard.

'It would not do to be unable to account for their property when they arrive to collect it,' said Vonn, 'so, we are confined and kept alive to meet a worse fate.'

'They've come half way around the galaxy to get you back. They value you, so you're not going to face punishment. We have assurances of your treatment. You crashed here. You weren't escaping,' said the guard. It sounded like a well-rehearsed and often repeated speech.

'How many of you are there? Are many confined?' I asked

'At this facility we are twenty, five of us are confined.' He shrugged, repeating his odd one shouldered gesture. 'I do not know how many of us are to be returned, but it does no good to hide. Our once and future owners can read our blood trackers from orbit. There is no true escape except death.'

'You don't have time to deliver that in person. I need to meet a visitor at 5:00pm and you can't be here unescorted.'

I followed the guard back to my car. Vonn, still holding the cake, watched as we walked the length of the corridor.

71

Outside, the sky still held brooding grey clouds, but the rain had stopped. The air was humid and heavy with evaporating surface water.

'I still don't understand how we can just hand them back. Slavery is illegal. Even I know that much about human rights.'

'And there you have it. They aren't human,' he said. 'I'm not saying I agree but would you rather we start an interplanetary war with a more advanced civilisation over a few hundred aliens who only crashed here a decade ago?'

I didn't have an answer for that, so I fumbled for the keys as we crossed the car park and pressed unlock on the remote.

'What makes you think they won't just enslave us as well?'

'Vonn's people believe they will hold the terms.'

'What did he mean, "a legal basis to remain"?' I asked.

The guard sighed and hung his head, 'You're not supposed to know.' He said as he closed the door.

I started the engine and opened the window. 'But?'

'They're only taking back the unmarried ones.

'You do know we're just for show, right. Us guards, they'd wipe the floor with us even with the control rods. We here to keep people out not in. The aliens stay by their own choice. Only the suicidal ones are confined, and we didn't do that either.'

As I reached the main gates, a sleek red convertible arrived. The 5:00pm expected guest I guessed. The driver was a woman with a perfect mane of blonde hair, dark glasses and lips that matched her car. I idly wondered why she was there, then drove home and straight past it, heading to Fran's house.

It was past 6:00pm when I arrived, and I almost thought better of the idea, but Fran had led the LWC campaigning 'Aliens are people too.' If she knew there was a loophole to save them, she would know the best way to exploit it.

A few hours later, after confirming the information (don't ask how), I sat on Fran's chintz sofa clutching a Queen's pattern china cup and saucer of tea and a custard cream watching her network. We might not be mumsnet or the W.I. but the LWC still had clout.

'So, Doreen dear, can I leave you to arrange the speed dating evenings?' Fran paused momentarily, 'Oh I'm planning a series of blind dates. I'm sure Trudy will do it.'

My blood ran cold and I choked on my custard cream. Surely, she wasn't expecting *me* to go on a date.

'I have to go dear, Trudy's choking and she's gone a terrible puce colour.' She hung up her phone. 'Are you alright dear?'

'No.' I replied.

'Shall I fetch some water? A pat on the back perhaps?'

'I'm fine,' I replied. 'No. I refuse. I'm not speed dating, blind dating or any other sort of stupid idea you might have. Just …no.'

'I thought you wanted to help them?'

'I've made the LWC aware of the loophole. Now it can be publicised and anybody who feels they could marry an alien,' I paused and shuddered involuntarily thinking of Vonn's huge zombie like appearance and those scars, 'can approach them and see if they are willing.'

'What do you mean willing? Why wouldn't they be?'

'Well, quite apart from the difference in species and attraction considerations, aren't they just swapping one form of slavery for another?'

'What a dreadful thing to even think, let alone say. I'm disappointed in you Trudy.'

'Goodnight Fran.' I said and let myself out. I was still surprised at my temporary ability to say 'No' and I hoped her disappointment would be sufficient for her to leave me out of any arrangements she made, because I doubted the skill would last.

73

The next day Facebook and Twitter were alive with the news as was the TV. I felt sure that now people were aware, enough women would come forward that all the eligible aliens could find a wife if they wanted. My involvement was not required and over.

Until I opened my door to fetch in the milk and found Fran on my doorstep. I strongly considered closing it again, but that was cowardly. She was an eighty-year-old woman. 'I hope you've had time to reconsider your opinions young lady,' she said in lieu of a greeting.

'No.' I said, exceedingly pleased to have kept my resolve overnight.

'What a selfish attitude.'

'Yes, it is,' I said and smiled, 'I'd make a terrible wife and I find them hideous.'

Fran straightened her spine and rested both hands on her walking stick. 'Then I feel we can't be friends.'

I felt a small pang of sadness at her words. Fran had been the first person to welcome me to the LWC. However, I refused to allow her to bully me anymore.

'Good bye then Fran.' I picked up my milk and closed the door.

I hadn't even put the door chain back into place before she rapped, three times on the door with the handle of her cane.

I sighed and undid the lock again. 'Yes Fran?'

'Good on you girl. I was beginning to think you were bit of a damp squib. Glad to see you have some backbone after all.'

'Fran, what do you want?'

'I want you to help organise my blind dates. I'm getting a bit old for this much activity.'

I waited for her to continue, and I wasn't disappointed.

'All right, I confess, I wanted you to take part. But, I need you to help me organise things and run me around. Will you do that?'

'Yes, but I will *only* be involved in the organising. Have you even asked if they want to take part?'

'Make yourself presentable girl, that's our first destination.'

I tried not to feel hurt. In my opinion, I was presentable. I'd showered and dressed in clean jeans without holes. What more did she want?

'You'd better come in. I'm not driving over there before coffee.'

In the end we were delayed by a few hours as Fran took telephone calls from the press and venues which had offered free meals and activities for the blind dates. Although the venues were very generous, I would've bet Fran had bullied or guilted most of them into it. She was very good at getting other people to do what she wanted. I was no exception. She wasn't done with me and I knew it.

While she was otherwise occupied, I baked to give us an excuse to visit the facility again. Using the ingredients to hand I managed sausage rolls and quiche alongside Victoria sponge cakes and chocolate chip cookies. There was a reasonable donation when I'd finished but now I needed to change again as I was dusted with flour.

'Do you own a dress dear?'

I let her have this argument, but only because I didn't have any clean jeans, honest. I brushed my hair too, but I wasn't putting makeup on.

We arrived at the facility to find news vans and journalists congregated around the entrance along with groups of placard waving and chanting protesters. I stopped beside the sentry box and wound down my window to speak to the guard, the same one as before, only to have a microphone shoved rudely in my face.

'Are you here to choose an alien husband?'

I opened my mouth to speak, but Fran had leaned over. 'No comment,' she said. The journalist withdrew as the guard advanced. 'Loxington LWC baked goods donation,' I said.

'Hello,' he said, 'Sorry, didn't recognise you all dressed up. You remember the way?' He winked at me and opened the gate.

It was a straight drive to the main building, so I could scarcely lose my way. I chose not to take offence. The guard who met us in the parking area was also the same man as before. He opened Fran's door and assisted her to get out, she blushed like a schoolgirl.

'What have you unleashed on us?' he asked as we walked down the long, gloomy corridor. 'Every facility has journalists, protesters for alien rights, protesters against alien rights, protesters against alien-human marriage and heaven only knows what else.'

'Are you still getting cake donations?' I asked.

'No, the table's looking a bit bare.'

'It's a good job we brought these then isn't it?'

As before, the dining room was deserted. I noted the depleted goody table and left the unfortunate guard to Fran's directions on the correct way to present the cakes. Poor man.

This left me at liberty to look down the corridor as I expected at least one of the aliens to inspect us. I wasn't disappointed. Now I knew why I hadn't heard Vonn approach last time. An alien dropped soundlessly from the shadows above the door, where he'd been watching us. Vertical-slitted pupils, one of the best adaptations for low-light ambush predators, ask any cat.

'Perhaps we should bring you guys shirts and shoes instead of food.' I said. This one wasn't Vonn. His scarring was far less severe, but he still only wore cropped trousers. 'Aren't you cold?'

'The temperature is not extreme enough to incapacitate and comfort is not a requirement.'

'Oh my.' Fran stared open-mouthed at the alien. 'Trudy said you were large and intimidating, but I think she understated it.'

'So now you believe me,' I said, shaking my head in mock reproach.

'You have returned with more cake little mouse?'

This time I didn't jump when Vonn spoke from behind me. I'd seen his shadow on the floor.

'Are you also responsible for supplying what we need?'

'You needn't blame me, I'm barely involved.'

'Why are you here then, if not for a marriage partner?'

'She brought me dear,' said Fran. 'The LWC are arranging speed dates and blind dates. I need to know how many of you wish to take part.'

'Eighteen, all except my brother and I.'

'Why isn't your brother interested?' Fran asked.

'If he were free to choose he would be, but he is already married.'

'And you? Are you married too?' She asked.

'No.' His tone of voice closed the conversation. I wondered if he could teach me to stop Fran in her tracks so effectively.

'That sounds like neither of us wants to be damned by an "I do",' I said.

'Trudy you're a wicked girl,' said Fran, her lips pursed like she'd sucked on a lemon.

Vonn and I both laughed. His fangs very prominent.

'Doesn't the fact he's married mean he doesn't have to return?' I asked.

'She is an overseer, they must both return.'

'You're very brave choosing to return at his side. You must love him very much.'

Vonn didn't reply. He stared at me and swallowed a few times then turned to the food table. 'There is no lemon cake,' he said.

77

'I didn't have any lemons left.'

'It is good, I didn't like it.'

'Don't eat anything from this new batch dear, she made all of them,' said Fran.

'Thank you for the warning.' Vonn replied, and bowed to her.

'Everyone's a critic today. Shall we get on with this?'

Sidar was the only one left on suicide watch. The others had regained hope on hearing there was a chance of reprieve. With the slave ship less than three months away. I wondered how real their chances were to find true love and marry in such a short time-frame, then smiled at my fancy. Love has never been a requirement, just an understanding. The aliens gained a right to remain, but what would the brides want or get in return?

We set the event date for Saturday and arranged with the guard for chaperones for the speed dates. The aliens would decorate the hall at the facility and we would arrange a coach to bring interested girls over.

'Will you bring lemon cake next time?' Vonn asked.

'I'm hoping there won't be a next time.'

The next week passed very quickly. I awoke to texts and emails of instructions from Fran and Doreen, carried out my day job and came home to another list of tasks for the evening, and then I was required to ferry Fran about.

By Saturday morning all that could be arranged had been. I have no idea where the LWC found their female participants, but the coach was full. The only criteria, the women were eligible to marry. There were pretty girls in their twenties through to Fran and Doreen in their eighties, all supposedly out to bag a husband. Tonight, I wasn't sure which party were the predators and I almost felt sorry for the husbands to be.

Then came the blind dates, drawn on the speed dating evening. I don't know how the women got to the venues, but I didn't get to realise my hope not to go to the alien facility ever again. I drove over with Fran, collected the prey and returned him at the end of the evening and, on a few occasions, earlier, if the date went badly or didn't show at all.

Every time we went I met Vonn and a different alien. By the end of the month I knew all eighteen who sought wives, but I hadn't met Sidar. The opportunity had never been offered again.

I didn't know what to make of Vonn and was glad I didn't have to prolong the meetings much longer. I found him repulsive to look at, intimidating and offensive, but I didn't keep making comments about his faults. It was obvious he cared deeply for his brother and for the rest of his people. He'd developed a rapport with the guards and even with Fran. But me, he never failed to find something to insult about me. My looks, my clothes, my cooking and my behaviours were all up for comment and scrutiny. Between him and Fran I was truly, Trudy the miserable.

Each of the alien males dated several women at once. To my surprise, a dozen of the local couples were going steady after only two months. In preparation, everyone involved had already applied for and received 'Certificates of No Impediment' and a joyous joint celebration at the facility was planned for the week before the slave ship was scheduled to arrive. A registrar had agreed to officiate the unusual wedding, one of several occurring around the country on the same day.

It was a lot more cost effective than unique weddings. My part of the organisation was flowers. I ordered silk bouquets and fifty table decorations to match. They were in storage somewhere in the facility.

Most of the members of LWC were providing food for the wedding buffet but I'd opted out. I'd had enough comments about my food, thanks very much. I paid towards the fizz for the toast instead. They'd ordered quite a few magnums of prosecco and I'd paid the deposit.

It was a Saturday night with a month to go. A dozen humans and aliens sat around a table discussing colour schemes for decorating the hall. One LWC member suggested rose pink and white sashes and chair backs. Fran vetoed that proposal. 'No dear, I don't want to clash or blend in with the decorations.'

Fran was almost giddy with excitement at the prospect of the upcoming nuptials. 'I have a beautiful cream pillbox hat decorated with pink and cream roses and net. It goes so well with my dress.' Then turning to me she said, 'When are you available to shop for your ensemble dear? I suppose I need to go with you, so you don't choose something totally unsuitable.'

I sighed. I'd started looking for suitable rental property, outside of walking distance of the LWC. Almost anything would be better than this. Even as I formed the self-pitying thought, I looked at Vonn and felt guilty. At least I had the freedom to leave.

'That isn't necessary, thank you.'

'But dear – '

'But nothing. I won't be attending. Is there anything else that needs discussing, or can we go home?'

The meeting ended. I drove Fran home and dropped her off. I have no idea who was giving and receiving the cold shoulder treatment, but I was glad for the silence.

Sunday morning found me up early for once, searching on the internet for property within fifteen miles of my office. There was a surprisingly small choice available outside of Loxington.

By lunchtime I'd narrowed my choice down to three properties. Only one I particularly fancied though, and I decided to arrange a viewing for the two-bedroomed first floor flat with a balcony, close to a park and within walking distance of work, a pub and some local shops. I printed the details and put them on the table ready to call the estate agent on Monday evening.

Three sharp knocks sounded on the front door. I'd come to recognise the Fran summons. I couldn't really ignore her. My car was outside, so she knew I was here. Sighing, I made my way to the door, braced and opened it to find it wasn't Fran at all.

'May I visit with you little mouse?'

At least he was fully clothed. I wondered what would happen if I said no. I couldn't physically prevent him from coming inside.

'I am sorry to visit without an appointment. Would you prefer I return later?'

'I'd prefer you didn't return at all,' I said as I stepped away from the door.

The alien passed through the frame, just, by ducking his head. I lead him into the kitchen. He sat at the table, making my room seem tiny. I made coffee and sat opposite him to drink mine.

'What do you want?'

'To talk, is all.'

'So, talk.'

'You do not like me.' It wasn't a question, so I didn't bother trying to deny his observation. 'Will you tell me why?'

'Because you don't like me. You insult me at every opportunity.'

'You will not shed tears when I am gone.'

'I don't know whether I'll cry, but I'll feel sorry for all of you who have to go back. Nobody should live as a slave.'

He ran his hands through his midnight hair, leaned his head forward and closed his eyes. When he spoke, his voice was almost a whisper. 'I am sad you will not be at the wedding. I feared you would not return to the facility, so I came here to speak.' He looked … sad. 'Thank you. From all of us, thank you very much.'

'You're welcome.' A thought occurred to me. 'It's Sunday. How did you get here?'

'How are those statements linked?' Vonn asked. 'Our spaceship crashed.'

'Ha, ha, very funny I'm sure. I just realised, it's Sunday so there aren't any buses running past the facility and I didn't hear a car. Did you walk?'

He didn't answer, simply looked at me and blinked.

'If you think you can fit, I'll run you back in my car.'

'Why?'

'Because you walked fifty miles just to say thanks. I'll grab my coat.'

We travelled in silence, but it was the companionable sort. Neither of us felt the need to fill it. I dropped him at the main gate and turned around to head back. The guards waved frantically at the car and ran into the road to stop me.

'What the …'

'We got the message a few hours ago, but nobody knew where Vonn was. The slave ship will be here tomorrow evening.'

'Vonn. You need to call Fran and Doreen at the LWC, tell them what's happened. They'll need to gather any girls that want to get married here tomorrow morning, then get your people there at the same time, preferably dressed.'

'You are leaving?' Vonn asked.

'Nope, I'm going to make use of these journalists around the gate. Let's give them a story.'

I passed on the news and within minutes we were receiving Tweets and Facebook messages. We needed someone authorised and willing to carry out the wedding ceremonies in the morning both for our facility and all the others.

Some individuals are OK I guess, but mostly people sucked. I had to admit that sometimes they can be amazing. It took less than an hour for our planned registrar to contact us and confirm she would be there. The weddings would happen provided the couples arrived and said their vows.

It was hard to believe that in less than a day any unmarried aliens would be gone. Proof of alien existence had come crashing into our lives a decade ago in a big way, quite literally. The scenes of the mothership breaking through the atmosphere and streaking across the London sky made TV news and newspaper headlines the world over.

In these days of cell phones and YouTube, the authorities could not have hidden the event even if they'd tried. They couldn't have hidden the devastation either as the huge spacecraft crashed down in St James' Park and ploughed its way as far as Parliament.

Bystanders say the impact felt like an earthquake or a bomb. Ten humans died in the incident and many hundreds were injured. Buildings a mile away suffered damage. Yet the ship survived more or less intact and so did most of her passengers.

The crew perished, suffocating when the hull breached. It must have been a terrible death. To be so far from home and wonder if your soul would find its way home to your distant gods and stars.

When the first of the passengers awoke from stasis and the rows upon rows of coffin like stasis chambers disgorged their contents, the emergency services staff feared they would suffer a similar fate. But the thousands of large and powerful humanoids must have been destined for a world with an atmosphere compatible with ours. Some were injured and all of them were afraid and unable to communicate with us.

The rest is history, so they say. Our newest refugees were aliens of the extra-terrestrial sort and couldn't be shipped home. They learned and assimilated our culture scarily fast, so they told us of the slavery and brutality, but we failed them and sold them short when their masters came calling.

I'm one of the cowards that allowed this to happen. I didn't make my leaders do what was right. Monday was my chance to vindicate myself and keep as many of these people as possible from forced repatriation as slaves.

The morning dawned bright and beautiful and far too early. I wished it could have been a little less shiny because it hurt my head. We'd spent the entire night decorating the hall, erecting and decorating a huge gazebo for the ceremony, arranging furniture, and preparing a buffet. Now I'd done my part and I wanted to curl up in a corner and sleep for a few hours before I could even think of driving home.

It wasn't happening. Everybody wanted something from me. A sound bite, confirmation a dress looked OK, was the bouquet the right way up (as if I would know). It was these people's wedding day, so a surly grunt wasn't acceptable. They deserved some time and a smile.

When the time came, eighteen couples stood before the assembled guests and took their oaths in accordance with our laws. It was done.

Among the guests were Fran and Doreen. We acknowledged each other but made no attempt to speak. The woman with the red convertible and lipstick was also there. She was tall and graceful. Red suited her, even if it wasn't appropriate for most weddings. We weren't introduced, and the aliens pointedly ignored her, so she sat at the front on the bride's side, next to Fran. The oddest thing was she never removed her sunglasses. I guessed she'd forgotten her ordinary ones.

I sat at the back of the gazebo by choice, on the groom's side by invitation, feeling scruffy in my jeans and t-shirt. I'd not had time to go home and change, so I was the most underdressed person in the room. If you didn't count Sidar who made a surprise appearance and sat beside Vonn, on the front row, dressed only in cut-offs.

The vows had been said and the registers were being signed, so the guests began mingling before we went inside to eat. I'd almost made my way to Vonn for my introduction to Sidar, when his brother saw the woman in red. He started yelling something in his own language. I couldn't understand the lingo, but the manner was aggressive.

Vonn tried to lead him away from the gazebo, but Sidar wouldn't move. He stilled as she walked towards him. When she reached him, she slapped Sidar across the face and removed her sunglasses, revealing vertical-slitted pupils.

'I'd hoped the make-up would fool you a little longer Sidar,' said the only female alien I'd seen, 'but no matter husband dearest.'

He didn't reply.

'Come, is that any way to greet your wife?' she asked and smiled: beautiful but cold and cruel. 'It seems I must teach you your place again before the ship arrives.' She withdrew a pen shaped cylinder from her bag and twisted it.

The cylinder began to glow and hum. Both aliens retreated. I had no idea what the cylinder was or what it did, but the extra distance didn't seem to help any.

She pointed it at Sidar. Vonn stepped in front of him and screamed in pain. Nothing had appeared to leave the rod, but blood poured from a wound on his chest I hadn't seen inflicted.

'Kneel Sidar and I will turn off the rod.'

'No.' Vonn croaked, collapsing on his stomach.

Sidar wobbled and turned as if to run. He looked at his brother and knelt before his wife. He had made some sort of decision that let him reach an inner peace. He raised his chin, nodded at me and smiled. 'He speaks of you often Little Mouse,' he said, 'please care for him.'

Too late the guards reached us. Sidar's hand shot forward almost faster than I could follow. He grabbed the woman's arm and forced the rod up under his chin, stabbing it like a knife through the soft tissue and into his brain.

He convulsed once, and I watched the life leave Sidar's eyes as he crumpled onto the ground. The sound of Vonn's screams changed, even as he rolled and caught his brother's falling body. The woman hadn't turned the rod off and now it was inside Sidar's head. I grabbed the end of the rod from Sidar's chin and fighting nausea as it vibrated between my fingers, I pulled it from the wound.

The guards lead Sidar's wife away, most probably for her protection, until the ship came to remove her.

Help arrived in the form of two elderly LWC members who began to staunch Vonn's bleeding.

In his voice hoarse Vonn said, 'twist it.'

I twisted. The rod stopped. Before me were two sets of dead eyes. One set beyond any help the other set only wished to be. Vonn closed Sidar's eyes.

I knew exactly how I'd ended up in these situations. It's the same reason I can't visit an animal re-homing centre unaccompanied. I can't help myself. I can't stand to see any living creature give up hope.

'Vonn I'm sorry,' I said. He didn't respond. I hadn't expected him too. He was in shock and denial and grief and pain.

'They can't hurt him or take him back now. They can only take you.' It was too soon, and it was wrong, but it had to be now. There was no love and very little like on either side. This wasn't how I imagined or wanted, but I could help, and he needed it. 'Vonn, will you marry me?'

He stared up at me and blinked. 'What did you say?'

'Will you marry me?' I repeated.

He didn't take any time to think. 'Yes.'

After a little confusion and persuasion, everybody resumed their seats and the poor registrar repeated the ceremony for two dishevelled and bloodstained people. And just like that it was over, and we were married. Neither of us had planned it. Neither wanted it and neither was ready.

I left the cleaning of the facility to the LWC and drove home alone. Vonn spent the remainder of his wedding day and his wedding night in the hospital under sedation, for which I was very grateful as there was only one bed in my house and I was not going to share it with him.

The terms didn't insist on marriage forever, but we would have to live together and stay married for 12 months to keep Vonn safe. Then we could have a nice civilised divorce or annulment or something and everybody would be happy.

Sleeping arrangements, rather than not wanting to be part of Loxington, decided my next few days activity. I left Vonn in the facility until all the tenancy paperwork was agreed for the two-bedroom flat I'd found and hired a van. I had no shortage of strong aliens to carry all my things for me. It was the easiest move ever.

It was wrong of me, but I'd avoided Vonn. I already knew it had been a mistake born of good intentions and a justified fear of slavery. I was afraid to face him, afraid to share my space with him and in all honesty afraid *of* him. What if he expected or wanted the *whole* marriage deal?

As far as I was concerned we were married in name only. He could do whatever aliens did and I would carry on my life as before. There would just be the inconvenience of a shared bathroom. And having to share my life, kitchen and lounge with a virtual stranger who enjoyed insulting me.

Finally, I'd run out of good excuses, so I went to collect my husband. I found him seated in the dining room, waiting. His posture slumped and weary, but he managed a half-hearted smile and a greeting. 'Hello Trudy.'

'Morning.' It was better than little mouse. 'Are you ready to go?'

The drive to our new flat was a little strained. I didn't know what to say to him and he didn't speak. I didn't know what he was thinking but it was Sidar's funeral after lunch, and he must have been mourning the loss of his brother. He might have reflected on the changes to his marital status too. I know he didn't look happy.

I parked in the designated space and waited while he climbed out of the car. He didn't have much physical baggage I could help with. Just a big holdall. Not much to show for 10 years on Earth. Now probably wasn't the time to ask either. I didn't know when would be.

We took the stairs slowly and I unlocked the door.

'Should I carry you over the threshold?'

'No thanks, you should be careful of your stitches.'

The flat was tiny and the grand tour lasted three minutes. The last two rooms, the bedrooms, were opposite each other and my suitcase sat on the floor between them.

'Which room?' I asked.

There were of a similar size with comparable furniture in both, but I hadn't made the beds in either room. I'd expected him to arrive with his own bedding. He would have to put up with my girlie duvet covers until he bought his own.

He looked in both rooms and gave his strange one-shoulder shrug. 'It doesn't matter.'

'OK.' I dragged my suitcase through the door of the room to the right. My heart was in my mouth when he followed me inside and sat on the dressing table stool, which creaked ominously. He clutched his holdall like a teddy bear as he watched me make my bed and unpack my suitcase.

When I opened the door to the second wardrobe and began hanging coats, he looked around as if he'd missed something and asked, 'Where shall I put my things?'

'In your wardrobe.' He stared at my second head. 'It's in your room with your bed across the hall'

'I thought married humans shared a bed.'

'Well you thought wrong, so you'd better go and unpack. I'll bring you some bedding in a minute.'

It was closer to ten minutes, but I found him sat on his dressing table stool with his head in his arms on the dressing table. His still full bag lay at his side. I dropped the bedding on the mattress and put my hand on his shoulder. 'Are you OK?'

He shuddered at my touch, so I withdrew my hand.

'Why did you marry me?' he asked, his voice tiny.

'Because it was the only way I could save you from deportation, or whatever they're calling it.'

'You don't wish to be married to me?'

'I don't know you well enough for me to be really happy about the situation, but I'm hoping we can remedy that and become friends. If not, we should manage to house-share until we can safely get divorced.'

'I was worried I would disappoint you, but you have the end already in sight... I will try to be a good housemate.'

'Would you like a coffee?'

He shook his head, so I made up his bed and left him to his thoughts. Later I knocked on his door to check he was ready for the funeral. He hadn't moved.

'Vonn, it's nearly time to go.'

He moved like a Victorian automaton, none of his grace remained, but he followed me from the flat and down the stairs to the car. We were going to meet at the crematorium. Perhaps we should have had a funeral procession from the facility to the crematorium, but Vonn had not wanted to.

The day was warm and bright and the scenery pleasant. I felt guilty for enjoying the drive, but I had not known Sidar and felt only a sadness for his passing, not real grief. I worried for Vonn. He'd been prepared to give up everything for his brother and now he was alone. I couldn't even begin to imagine what they'd been through together or how Vonn felt now. I didn't know how to support him either. But perhaps we could talk.

'Did you live far from here after you first arrived?'

'No.'

'Did Sidar work here on Earth?'

'No.'

'How about you?'

'No.'

'Do you have any human friends from before?'

'No.'

I had no business feeling hurt, but I felt rejected from Vonn's single word answers, so I drove the rest of the way in silence. I would be there if needed but I would not force myself where I wasn't welcome.

The LWC were in attendance of course, and the now married couples too. The guards from the facility and other facility staff were there too, but nobody from his 10 Earth years before. Sidar must have known people and made friends. It was hard to believe nobody had come to pay their respects.

A month passed by. Vonn was true to his word about being a good housemate. He didn't make a mess or any noise. He didn't offer to cook, but he ate whatever I cooked without complaint and he didn't hog the bathroom. He just never spoke to me more than, 'Could you pass the salt please' or to answer a question with brevity to the point of rudeness. It became harder to believe we could become friends.

I now lived within walking distance of work, albeit a long walk. I told myself it was to improve my fitness and save money, but I walked mainly because it took longer, and I would have to spend less time in the flat.

It was always the flat, never home. Vonn found a job in house removals where his size and strength were an asset and took all the work offered, normally leaving early in the morning and returning late in the evening. We rarely sat in the same room or even ate at the same time.

I don't know how he felt, but I was lonely and sad. I told myself he was grieving, and tired from his strenuous job. He likely was, but he also didn't want to spend time with me. He didn't call me a little mouse. He didn't insult me or tease me either, and my summer passed in silence.

I wasn't the sort to sleep with any stranger but living with the coldness felt like a punishment. Should I have invited him to my bed that first night? Was this distance my fault? Most importantly, did I want to remedy our lack of friendship or endure until the marriage could end? The questions and their lack of answers upset me.

'We never do anything. Would you like to go to the cinema this weekend?' I asked at breakfast one morning. 'Or we could go for a meal or a drink.'

Vonn stopped eating and raised his head. I smiled at him, but he looked straight through me, his expression blank. 'I do not wish to go out.' He didn't say it but I'm sure I heard the missing *with you* anyway. 'Go with your friends.'

Even if I'd had anybody else to go with, I didn't feel right socialising without him. He might regret it, but we were married. The stress was beginning to eat at me and I had difficulty sleeping. I decided that perhaps I should move out. We needn't tell anybody, so he would still be safe from the slavers. I had felt less lonely when I lived alone.

Vonn came home later and later. When he was there he rarely left his room and avoided all attempts at conversation. One evening he walked in at 11pm, took his dinner from the fridge and went to his room, without even heating it first.

Feeling dejected, I curled up in my chair and read from my favourite book with just the light from the street lamp outside. I'd re-read it so often over the past few months most of the pages were no longer attached and I often skipped to my favourite parts. The happy-ever-after bits. I fingered the leaflet I used as a bookmark, too afraid of the outcome to make the opportunity to raise the problem with Vonn, and looked towards Vonn's door.

Half an hour later, Vonn crept out of his room. I watched him cross the passage and raise his hand to knock on my door, only to let it fall back to his side. Then I noticed the holdall at his side and I realised he was leaving. Just walking out.

I hoped he had somewhere safe and warm to live. I wouldn't cry. Nor would I ask him to stay or why he was leaving. He was as unhappy as I felt and asking him to stay would be unfair. But I would call him to task for sneaking away without having the decency to say goodbye.

Head bowed Vonn walked past me. I was as unnoticeable as the little mouse he'd once called me what seemed a lifetime ago. He opened the door and walked through, only to stop and kneel in the doorway. His shoulders shook with silent sobs.

'Why the middle of the night? I'm not keeping you a prisoner, so why leave like this?' He jumped out of his skin and turned to face me. 'You've made it clear enough you don't like me, and we can't hold a conversation, but this is a little extreme.

'Do you just want me to worry about you? Because you're a little late. I've been worried for months. But sneaking off without even a goodbye is mean and low.'

Vonn came back inside and closed the door. He leaned against it heavily and slid down until he sat on the floor. Tears rolled down his cheeks and he didn't bother to wipe them away. 'I'm broken inside and I do not know what to do. I see the pain I cause you. It adds to my shame, but I cannot be different. I do not know how. Our marriage is voidable, we have not consummated it. If I leave, you will have your life back.'

'Vonn, if you don't want to live with me fine. But marriage only ends when a court says. Couples remain legally married, even if they live apart.'

'Leaving you doesn't terminate the contract?' He asked.

I school my head. 'It doesn't matter how much you regret it or how sad you are. You can't get out of this that easily. We're married for better or worse and we're having the worse. No relationship will work without effort from both sides, not even a friendship but you don't even want to try.'

'You are wrong, but I do not know how.'

'It starts with talking. I think you need to do a lot of it and not just with me.' I gave him my bookmark, a leaflet for bereavement counselling I'd been too afraid to give it to him. 'I think you need help.'

He looked at the leaflet. 'I am afraid.'

'Would you like me to come with you?'

He smiled. It was only a ghost of his fanged first smile, but it was real. 'I would like that very much.'

I think that was when the hope began to return to his eyes.

Flash Fiction Competition 2018

This year saw our first internal writing competition. The anonymously submitted short stories were read aloud at the June 2018 writers group and the listeners scored the stories under these headings with a simple binary **1** or **0**

- Did the story engage you from the outset?
- Was the story enjoyable?
- Did the story have an interesting plot?
- Was the story easy to understand?
- Were the characters engaging?
- Did the story move at a good pace?
- Did the story contain interesting language?
- Did the story have at least one surprising plot element?
- Was the end satisfying?
- Was the end credible?

All seven entries are featured in this section. The placed stories are:

First	Death Wish by Carol Ritson
Second	The Story of a Bear by Patrick Bird
Third	Spring Fervour by Bob Mynors

Death Wish

Carol Ritson

As Sheriff Don Bronson's left hand gripped Josh's throat tightly, slamming him hard against the wall of the prison cell, his other hand clenched into a fist. He'd always known the young man was trouble, and now it was time to teach him a lesson.

The sheriff hissed in his ear, "What the hell was running through that tiny mind of yours while you were doing over a hundred miles an hour on the main high street? Did you think it was a laugh? Some sort of big joke?"

"I honestly wasn't thinking anything, Sheriff. I was drunk. I was too drunk to realise what was happening. I just vaguely remember my car mounting the sidewalk and the next thing I knew I was hitting these people"

The sheriff's face blazed red with fury as he shook his fist inches from the youth's cheek.

Josh baited him, offering no resistance. "Go ahead, sir, I deserve it," he said. "I was hoping that someone would have the guts to do it. Just pleased it's you, I'm sure you'll make it as painful as you can."

"Too right I will, son, you little ....!"

Don pushed Josh across the room and slammed him into the bars, with Josh's spine making contact with the metal frame. Winded, but not hurt, the young man brushed himself down and confidently strode towards Don, and goaded,

"Was that supposed to hurt? A child could have done me more damage than that!"

Don walked over and thumped him hard in the face sending him flying backwards against the bars.

"That," he spat, "is for killing my granddaughter!"

The floor became bloodstained as the young man wiped his nose with his hand. Keeping eye contact with the sheriff, he stood up slowly, and walked towards him.

"That's a bit more like it. Now how about one for your grandson?"

He took a second blow, another to the chin, sending him crashing to the floor.

"That one's for Sam," Don spat again.

Gasping heavily, Josh crawled to his knees, staying there for a few seconds before standing. Don waited before delivering another blow to Josh's face, making him collapse again in a heap.

"And that one's for my wife!" he said.

Josh groaned, before sluggishly grabbing the bars for support. After taking time to regain his breath, he pulled himself up into a crouching position where he stayed glancing at the floor for a few seconds.

Don cried in anger, "Stay down, Josh! Stay there!"

The young man turned and glared up at the sheriff. Without losing eye contact, he defiantly grasped the bars harder and continued in his effort to stand. Don walked towards Josh, grabbed his hair with both hands and brought his own knee up sharply to meet Josh's face. Josh gasped in pain and collapsed on the floor. His groans were louder and lasted longer this time, but he grasped at the bars in an effort to stand.

Don strode over and crouching in front of Josh grabbed at the metal bars at either side of Josh's head, shouting, "For God's sake. What part of 'stay down' do you not understand?"

Spitting blood at him from a now split lip, Josh, replied with contempt, "And what part of 'I deserve to die' do you not understand, pal?"

As Josh streaked his blood across his face with the back of his hand Don recognised the look of determination in the young man's eyes, but he also realised that behind the bravado lay desperation. Josh actually wanted someone to purge him of his guilt, he needed to forget how much sorrow and death he had caused. He really did want to die!

Don's eyes narrowed "You actually mean it, don't you?"

Josh hissed sarcastically. "Well, hallelujah, he's finally got it!"

Don hastily stood, turned and strode to the other side of the cell. Resting his forehead against the bars of the small window, he considered the situation. The hopeless voice from behind, broke his thoughts.

Josh sounded desperate, "I'm disappointed," he said. "I thought you of all people would have been able to finish the job. I want it all over and done with! I need to make the mental images of your family's faces against my windscreen stop! There's no escape! Whether I'm awake or asleep I see them. The thoughts just repeat and repeat, over and over and over again."

Don turned and saw Josh standing, his back supported by the wall. Their eyes locked firmly in contact.

Josh had long known Don Bronson to be a man who would turn pain into aggression, and from the look that was now on the sheriff's face, he knew he wasn't far from getting the punishment he wanted or needed.

"What's up, Sheriff, lost your guts?" the young man taunted.

In fury the back of the sheriff's hand made contact with Josh's face. "Screw you, Josh!" he screamed.

When the young man smiled at him, Don suddenly realised that once again he had taken the bait, so he walked away from him. "Screw you!" he shouted again.

"You know what? I had the ride of my life that evening," Josh said, tormenting Don further.

Too angry to stop himself, Don yelled as he charged at Josh with his shoulder, slamming the young man's face against the bars, with fists raining hard into Josh's body. As every violent blow continued to sting and burn, Josh gripped the cell bars tight. Unsuccessfully, the young man tried to forget his guilt and instead concentrate on how calm and freeing impending death felt, knowing that with each and every painful punch he received, came some release for Don from the guilt he felt at being unable to stop his family from getting killed.

Don finally slammed his fist into the floor. He then took the key out of his pocket, turned and walked away, towards the cell door leaving a sobbing and battered, bleeding mess of a body on the floor.

"I'm sorry! I didn't mean to do it!" Josh managed to cry through the choking blood and tears as the sheriff placed the key in the lock. "I really am sorry! I just can't stop the image of my car smashing into your wife and grand-kids! I hate myself so much right now that I wish that you had just killed me and got it over and done with."

Walking out of the room, Don locked the door behind him. "I'd be making it too easy for you if I'd killed you right now. I swear Josh, my boy, that I will do everything in my power to make sure that you stay alive and live with your guilt for the rest of your life. I'm also going to make sure you don't get the death penalty. I think living with your thoughts will be a bigger torture for you, than giving you the satisfaction of making them stop."

Suddenly Don's walkie-talkie crackled into life. The Sheriff's Deputy's voice sounded urgent.

"Sir!" said the Deputy "We've managed to review the CCTV tapes of the accident. It's not him! It's not Josh driving the car! I know you've been looking to get him on some charge or other for years, but he's not the one who's killed all your family! He was riding shotgun. I'm really, really sorry to have to tell you this Don, but it was your youngest daughter Ellie, who was driving the car. She's the one who killed them. The officers are round at your house right now picking her up."

Sheriff Don Bronson had thought that losing his wife and his two grandchildren was bad enough, but as he looked around him at the bloody scene that covered the cell from floor to ceiling, at the crumbled twisted body that lay sobbing on the floor and waited for his daughter to arrive at the station, he realised that hell was far bigger and more painful than he could ever have imagined.

The Story of a Bear

P J Bird

In this existence, you just never know what type of life you're going to have. If you ask any teddy like me they will tell you that there are only three things a teddy bear asks for from their existence; to be able to find a home, to be well looked after by someone caring and to get given a nice name.

When we were made, we'd learned some of the horrible stories of what had happened to previous teddys like us. Stories about the poor bears whose owners liked to pull their arms and legs off, and what happened to the poor bears whose owners didn't care for them anymore.

When it became my turn to take my place on the shop floor, I wondered about how long it would take for me to find my new home. How long would it take for somebody to notice me? Some of the bears in the shop had been taken there a long, long time before me, and yet they still found themselves without a new owner, a new family.

I was lucky. After only a few days in the shops, I was picked up by a young woman who looked me in the eye and smiled before taking me to the check-out.

On the journey home I realized that I had no idea as to what 'I' was going to be. Would I be a brother? A sister? Or a best friend? Would I get to live with someone who cared for their toys?

Once we reached 'home' I was quickly put into a carrier bag and placed in a cupboard. In it I could see different toys, all new with some gift bags and some wrapping paper. Inside one of the bags there was a badge with a big number '4' on it. It seemed like I was going to be a birthday present.

The young woman took me out of the cupboard just a few days later. She covered me in wrapping paper and put me on the table. It wouldn't be long until I got to meet my new-found friend.

"Happy Birthday Charlie" I heard the woman call out as she handed me over, still covered in the wrapping paper. I could feel hands eagerly tearing off the paper and before too long I was in the hands of a small boy.

I could see that the boy was smiling at me. "Thank you Mummy" he said to the woman. He was happy. That had to be a good sign.

"Do you have a name for him Charlie?" Mummy asked. This was it. The moment of truth. Would I get a nice name? I didn't want anything boring like 'Mr. Bear'

I noticed Charlie smile at Mummy again. "Henry" Charlie declared about me. "Henry Bear" before he gave me a massive hug.

I soon knew that with Charlie, I had got a best friend. He would take me everywhere with him. If he and Mummy went shopping, I went with them. If he and Mummy went to the dentist, so did I. If he and Mummy went on holiday, I was there.

We had many adventures together, whether it was exploring what was lurking in the back garden, through to looking at the mysterious tunnel where Mummy put the dirty clothes. We also got into trouble sometimes. I can remember Mummy being very cross with him when he went to play rather than put his other toys away like she'd asked.

"I'm very upset with you Charlie" she had told him.

Charlie pointed at me. "Henry went to play as well Mummy" he had told her.

"Well I'm very upset with Henry as well."

'Thanks pal,' I'd thought to myself.

For two years, we were inseparable. When Charlie started school, he would always give me a hug before he went to school and then another hug when he got home. Mummy had told him that if Charlie wanted to show how grown-up he was at school he would have to leave me at home sometimes.

It was not long after Charlie turned six that things went wrong.

It was Charlie's friend Sam's birthday party. All of the children in 'Class One' were there. As always, I would go where Charlie went, so off we went to the party. When we got there, Charlie went straight to Sam to say hello and 'happy birthday.'

"Have you brought your teddy?" asked Sam?

"It's not my teddy" Charlie tried to explain. "It's Henry." He could see that Sam and some of his other friends were looking at him strangely.

"Teddy bears are for babies Charlie" Sam told him.

"You're not a baby, Charlie, are you?" another friend asked,

"Baby Charlie, Baby Charlie" they chanted at him. I wanted to tell them to stop, to leave Charlie alone, but I couldn't because obviously a teddy bear can't speak.

Charlie rushed over to Mummy, trying not to cry. He quickly handed me over shouting, "teddy bears are for babies."

Mummy and I went home, and she put me on Charlie's bed, waiting for him to get home from the party. It had been different today, but I had no doubt we would be best friends again when he got back from the party, and that he would be able to tell me all about the fun that he and his friends had enjoyed.

Charlie walked into his room smiling. He was happy. That was good to for me to see.

But when he saw me, his face turned.

I could see that he was upset by something. Had his friends been mean to him because he had taken his teddy bear to the party?

When he picked me up, there wasn't a hug from him. That was strange. I could see him carrying me over to a box that he only opened to put in old toys that he never played with any more. I was worried. Charlie and I were best friends. He wouldn't put me in there, would he?

'Don't do this, Charlie' I wanted to say to him, but I couldn't say anything.

Opening the box, I could see him look at me in the eye. It was like he was looking at me for one last time.

"I'm sorry Henry but teddy bears are for babies" Charlie said as he dropped me into the box.

And then the lid slammed shut.

It was dark in the old toy box. I could see lots of toys that I hadn't seen for a long time. Toys that Charlie would have long forgotten that he actually had. Would that happen to me? Would I become a forgotten toy that Charlie didn't know he had? I just hoped that there would be a day when the box would be opened, and that Charlie would play with me once more.

I was so pleased when the box opened, but it still came as a bit of a surprise when it I found Mummy looking at me, rather than Charlie.

"Charlie, do you want me to take Henry Bear to the school jumble sale?"

I saw Charlie look at me. He seemed to have grown since I had last seen him. I hoped that he would say no. We were best friends. I wanted to stay at home.

Charlie seemed sad when he nodded. I was bundled into a small box and placed in the car. All the worries I had had in the shop long ago came back to me. Who would buy me? Who would look after me? Would they be kind?

When we got to the school, the toys in the box and I were placed on the table. I saw Charlie walking around, looking at the different toys on the table. I just hoped he would change his mind and take me home. I didn't want to leave him.

He picked me up. For a brief moment I thought he was going to ask Mummy for me to come home.

He hugged me before putting me down on the table again. Was this it? Goodbye?

A little girl looked at me, "Daddy, can I have that teddy bear? Please?"

The little girl picked me up whilst her Daddy paid the lady at the table. I could see her smiling at me. At that moment, everything seemed like it would be OK.

When she gave me her first hug, I could hear Charlie's voice. "Look after him" Charlie told her. "He's my best friend."

Spring Fervour

Bob Mynors

It was early May: the sun was out - a change from the deluge and smother of fog April had brought. The sky was startlingly blue. There were enough little fluffy-white cotton-wool clouds to make the sky vibrant, pretty, bright. Yet the daffodils, trumpets no longer shining, had heads already shrivelled, brown. The cherry blossoms, so soon rejected by their tree-hosts, lay already lost on the ground - pretty, pink, forlorn. Already the year, so recently new, was starting to die

The short walk to the shops felt almost too much for him today. "Come on," he thought. "This can't be right. I'm not old. Not that old." But even on this modest incline, he felt he needed to stop for a bit, not to catch his breath but to let blood surge back into his limbs with the energy to push him forward

♦ ♦ ♦

Despite the sun, despite the warmth, despite the evidence of recent days and of the long, detailed weather forecast she had heard on the radio, she put on her raincoat, the lightweight one, appropriate to the time of year with its floral pattern. She hated getting wet, and had been caught out too many times before, especially this year

She picked up her basket and looked for a notepad, then decided this would be a social trip not a shopping trip. There was nothing she actually needed, so a list would be a little redundant. If she saw anything she fancied, she would just buy it. Really she was going out to see the world, maybe have a chat with someone if she was lucky

♦ ♦ ♦

"Why, didn't I make a list?" he chided himself. "I've already forgotten what I came out for. I should always just jot down what I need and bring the list with me." So often he got half way home before remembering the main thing he had gone out to buy. It was always something basic and necessary - teabags, toilet rolls, stuff like that. The walk might be good for him, but the stress wasn't. So rather than rack his brain, he thought he would go and sit down near the shops for a bit of a ponder and make his list there. He never liked hanging round in the shops if he could help it

Then he realised he had nothing to write on. This made sitting and thinking about it even more important. He would have to sit down, think about what he had come out for and try to memorise it

When he rounded the corner and could see the shops, he saw also that the seat was already occupied - a woman in a raincoat. "What's she sitting there right in the middle for?" He recognised her – sort of. Sometimes they caught the same bus, bought groceries in the same shops. But he didn't know her. He didn't know her name. They had never spoken. "What's she sitting there right in the middle for?" he asked himself again. When someone is at one end of the seat, you were well with in your rights to sit at the other and ignore them. When they were in the middle and you sat next to them, you had to acknowledge them, even if the acknowledgement was a perfunctory one

♦ ♦ ♦

Using the laconic, understated, non-verbal communication the English are so good at, he approached the bench, nodded his slightest nod to the woman, smiled his thinnest, most wan smile at her and, with barely a movement of his hand but with a small eyebrow lift, asked wordlessly if anyone were already sitting there and would she mind if he did. Understanding the ritual implicitly, she smiled back and, again with a single hand gesture, granted permission

Sitting down did come as a relief and his first thoughts were simply to enjoy that. Then he remembered his task, remembered what he had come to the shops for. As he gathered his thoughts, his companion spoke. "Lovely day isn't it?"

This was what he had feared. He did not want conversation. He wanted to get on and get home. But he felt he could not just ignore her. "Better than we've been having," he replied. "Don't suppose it'll last though." Even as he said it, he knew the last bit was a mistake. It was an open invitation for her to respond

When it came - "Wasn't April a wash-out?" - it felt unremarkable enough for him to avoid further comment. But after a moment she added, "You live round here, don't you?" That could not be ignored without seeming rude, even though she was the one poking her nose in uninvited

"Just down the hill," was all he meant to say, but somehow his mouth wanted more. It added, "I've just come out to do some shopping and I've forgotten to make a list. I just sat down here to make sure I remember it all. I know I need cornflakes and washing up liquid, and I'd like some of those little oranges if they've got any. I can't think of anything else, but I'm sure there's something I'm missing."

The pair sat side by side in silence - a silence she broke. "Why don't you write your list now?" she asked. "Maybe if you can empty your mind of what you can remember, you'll make room for the things you've forgotten to come back to you."

He leaned forward and looked at her, perhaps a little dubious at the suggestion. "Do you think that'll work?"

"I don't know." An amused smile played across her lips, and into her eyes. "It might do. It might not. I've never tried it, so I can't say." Her smile grew a little wider, and she said, "But it can't hurt, can it?"

For the first time he looked at her closely and saw how lovely was her smile, how lovely were her eyes, how they shone slate blue. Never could he remember seeing such eyes before. He thought he would if ever he had. "It hardly matters though, because I've nothing to write on. Or with."

"Shame," she said. "Neither have I." Another silence ensued till she said, "I've an idea." She took a smartphone from her handbag, held it up. "Have you got one of these?"

He reached into his pocket. "Nothing that flash," he said, waving a small feature phone in front of her. "What do you want it for?"

"I don't want it. I want your number."

"Eh?" He didn't know where this was going but, falteringly, he recited, "OH - SEVEN," and the nine other digits.

"Now tell me what's on your shopping list. Cornflakes, was it?"

"What's the point …?"

"Don't argue. Just tell me what you want."

"Oh, all right." She's a bit bossy, this one, he thought. "Cornflakes. Oranges – those little ones that peel really easily."

"Oranges will do."

"Er – washing-up liquid. And cheese," he almost yelled. "Some cheddar cheese. That's what I've really come out for."

"… che-ddar che-ese." Looking up at him, she asked, "Anything else?"

"No. That's all."

The phone in his hand bleeped. "Aren't you going to get it?" she said

"It's stopped ringing. They've rung off."

"It wasn't a phone call. It was a text message. I've just sent you your shopping list. Do you know how to work that thing?"

"Not really. I don't know how to use it at all. My daughter keeps on at me, but it's only supposed to be for emergencies. Cheese is hardly an emergency."

"Let me show you what you need to do." She showed him where to find her message and how to open it. He read it off the screen. They closed it down then he opened it himself. He thought this was an achievement. "And if it ever makes that noise again, you'll know what to do. Yes?"

"Probably," he said, "but I don't suppose it will. It never has yet."

"What if it rings for a call? Do you know how to answer that?"

"Of course I do." He indicated the green button. "It's that one. But I don't get calls."

"Well, you never know," she said. "You might. Maybe today. After *Countdown*."

His eyes widened – and he leaned back

She grinned coyly behind one of those silly little finger-waves that some people do, and said "You won't mind? Will you?" then picked up her basket and left

He sat there, still, surprised. Had he just pulled? Had he just been pushed? Had the so nearly dying year just sprung back into life?

Que Calor!

Diane Bingham

A beautiful sunny July afternoon greeted the World Cup quarter-final. Gary was embarking on his football match ritual. Watch the game at a local pub, down a few pints, and a few more. Then home to sleep it off on the settee.

"Que Calor!" thought Jamie. He would have preferred to stay in and watch the game with his family. Crisps and pizzas provided by Mum and a few beers with Dad. But he had to do this.

Aloud he said, "Hot or what?"

"Too f***ing hot. Let's get to the f***ing pub," chunnered Gary.

Any response from Gary generally involved expletives never deleted.

"Hope this works," thought Jamie. He planned to marry Nancy, Gary's daughter.

"Please make him respect you," she'd pleaded. "It'll be so much easier for Mum. You know what he's like."

So, he had to impress him. But he had other less honourable motives. Beating Gary at his own game was very appealing. Maybe Jamie did have the masculine aggression and keen competitive edge that Gary so admired. Jamie was just more subtle and kept it well hidden.

Welcoming shouts and cheers heralded their entrance into the Black Bull.

Calls of, "Come on Gazza, time for a few pints."

"My shout Gary," said Jamie as he went to the bar. The barmaid smiled as she served Jamie, giving him a conspiratorial wink.

"Jamie, no messing with our Ella," Bill called out. "She's spoken for!"

Ella passed the pints across the bar. "Is this the first stop?"

"Aye, you're number one. Gary's got us down for three pubs this afternoon. Here, then a quick one …"

"… or two or three," hollered Gary, interrupting.

"… in the Swan, then it's over to the Red Lion," finished Jamie.

"Aye Ella luv, I want to see what this lad's made of. What with him wanting to marry my Nancy," shouted Gary.

Ella smiled at Jamie, "Quite a challenge you've got there."

Jamie took the drinks to the table. Gary grabbed his pint and downed it in three great gulps. "My turn Jamie lad."

"Just a half for me thanks. I've not finished this yet," said Jamie.

"A f***ing half? Only nancy boys drink halves and I'm not having a nancy boy for my Nancy!" trumpeted Gary and laughter broke out all round.

Ella pulled Gary's pint and passed it across the bar. "I'll bring Jamie's over. I need to clear that table."

Fifteen minutes and another round later the crowd were finishing their pints and heading out. Jamie grimaced as he forced the third pint down.

Next stop was the White Swan and a replay of the Bull, the only difference being the barmaid, Sally.

"That's Ryan's sister isn't it?" queried Fred.

"Aye, that family's got a monopoly on pubs round here. But they keep a nice pint," said Bill.

Jamie chatted quietly to Sally before bringing the drinks over. Then it was up and off to the next venue.

"Eng-er-land!" They chanted as they marched across the road to the Red Lion and the giant TV screen.

The landlord shouted, "Just in time lads, the pundits are up their own arses! The usual?"

"Yes, Tetleys for Fred and me and Fosters for the others," said Bill, walking over to the bar. Gary settled himself in the best seat; the prime spot for watching the game and ensuring everyone could hear his opinion of the pundits, the manager, the players and the 'f***ing Krauts'. Like a king in his castle he lorded it over the others. The term 'bully' didn't come near to describing the reality that was Gary.

"I'll give you a hand Bill," volunteered Jamie.

The landlord acknowledged Jamie with a cautious nod. "Long time Jamie."

"Yeh Ryan, I've been away at Uni and working in Spain."

"Local lad makes good heh?" smiled Ryan.

"For both of us, Ryan. We're a long way from St Mary's Comp. Nice to see you've got your own pub."

"Yeh, it's great being my own boss."

Ryan dropped his voice and mumbled quietly, "All thanks to you Jamie. Just glad I can return the favour at last."

Jamie thought back to the time he'd covered for Ryan. Not just covered for him but actually lied to the police. Still, he knew he'd done the right thing, giving him an alibi. Ryan had been tempted, or "led astray" as his mother would say, by Jason and that gang of no-hopers.

"No sweat Ryan. You weren't one of them."

"I know. I was stupid. I'd never have got a pub licence with a criminal record. Thanks again. I won't let you down and Ella will make sure I stay on the straight and narrow."

"I hear Jason didn't learn his lesson."

"No. He upped his game. His latest was armed robbery. Got seven years."

Then loudly Ryan said, "Did you know Ella's expecting?"

"Congratulations. That's great news." Jamie smiled and took the glasses over to the table.

He sat down to watch the game. Gary was in raptures, surrounded by his drinking buddies. He called them his 'mates', but really they were just blokes who were afraid to stand up to him.

All the men had well-reasoned opinions as to what Southgate, the manager, should do, who should be picked for the team and especially how England had made it to this stage of the competition. All different but all absolutely certain they were right, until Gary stepped in and overruled them with his incontrovertible footballing wisdom. No one dared challenge him.

"Boy, he's in his element," thought Jamie. Aloud he said, "You used to play, didn't you Gary?"

Yes, I was a f***ing demon full-back. No one got past me. Well, not in one piece they didn't," he snorted, spraying his close companions with lager.

The game started accompanied by roars from the pub crowd. A sad stalemate ensued until Muller scored a blinder a minute before half time. Groans and shouts of disbelief echoed round the pub as more pints were ordered.

"You can certainly hold your drink lad," said Bill.

"Lots of practice as a student," Jamie grinned.

Early in the second half Danny Rose headed in the equaliser. "Well he rose to the occasion," quipped Jamie, to grimaces all round.

"Why's Southgate's taking him off?" Gary asked.

Then Leighton Baines ran onto the pitch, slapping palms with Rose as he ran off. Gary was raging. "Baines only made the squad as a last-minute replacement. What's Southgate thinking?"

The stalemate continued. It was nail biting, but the tension reflected what was at stake, not the quality of the football. Then came the inevitable penalties.

Honours were even down to the final penalty.

Muller strolled to the spot, oozing confidence. Pickford dived and saved. From Gary and pals there were fists in the air, arms waving and shouts drowning out the TV.

Then Baines calmly stepped forward to face Neuer. "England waits," breathed the commentator. "Can the jinx be lifted?"

"Not Baines, not a f***ing Scouser!" screamed Gary.

Jamie glanced around and realised he was the only one actually watching. All the men had their eyes closed and their hands over their screwed-up faces. So as Baines started his run up to the ball Jamie felt as if he was in a kind of limbo, as if everything was frozen, time had stood still, and it was just he and Baines still functioning.

Baines stroked the ball firmly, precisely and straight into the top left-hand corner of the net. Jamie screamed. Yes, he realised he'd just screamed. And he was living the moment two seconds before everyone else, because he'd actually watched.

Gary was ecstatic. All the men jumped up and danced about, hugging each other. Tears very close to the surface. "We did it! Eng-er-land!"

Gary grabbed Jamie in a bear hug. "You're alright lad. You'll do. My God you can hold your own."

Jamie suddenly felt a deep affection for Gary. What was it? There was no affinity there. It was not empathy nor sympathy – no, he'd seen too often how Gary ruled the roost at home. Not a violent man but his mere presence was intimidating. So, what was it? It was an understanding. He'd experienced being in Gary's shoes and understood how it felt. Jamie's opportunities and chosen path were different. Recognising that difference on equal terms.

Jamie went to the bar. "Same again for everyone."

He beamed a wide smile that turned into a full throaty laugh, "But Ryan, could you make mine a Fosters? That non-alcoholic stuff is shite!"

Hook the Duck

Susan Allott

It was Saturday afternoon. The weather had turned warm, the mist had disappeared and now the sky was blue. The sun was a bright large yellow button pressed to on. I sighed heavily. Just what I didn't need. The fairground was filling up with excited children, dragging reluctant or nearly as excited parents, friends, grandparents etc.

What on earth was I doing here? What on earth was I thinking of saying yes for the local children's charity "Quackers" and dressing up as the biggest duck on earth, collecting money in a yellow bucket? Yes, even a yellow bucket.

I placed my furry webbed feet forward slowly, left then right, stop, breathe, left then right, stop, sit and plead for water from the small stall halfway across the grounds.

"Please can you hide me Wyn? I could sit at the back and pass you the water bottles from the fridge." I pleaded.

"Not on your Nellie," came a Welsh voice from within the gazebo. "Listen boyo, drink that water and get back out there. We've all got a job to do and yours is important. Your mam won't be pleased nor the boss. Okay, dieu, I'd smack your bum if I could find it."

With that small shake of the bones, I drank my water nearly in one go, placing the head back on and headed out onto the fairground. I was covered in fluff, yellow fluff, orange fluff. I sneezed three times and again heavily. I felt 'heavily'. I lurched forward trying to balance on my orange webbed felt feet. Wobble, wobble, left right, left right.

"Oh, what the heck," I thought to myself, spying a bench on the edge of the park near the bowling green. "Great." I tried to sit down as graciously as I could, sideways on like, not that easy when you have a big materially packed bum and large fluffy thing supposed to be a feathery tail!

"Steady Fred," I was telling myself, "easy now, one wing at a time. Made it.

"Hi Fred," a voice called out.

I moved my large duck head to where I thought the voice was coming from, I could just about see through the mesh eyes.

Again, "Hi Fred, what's with you?" the voice enquired full of laughter.

I recognised the voice coming from the candy floss stall.

"Huh," I mumbled, "oh - er - fine Sid, bit warm though."

"Go on with yer, it's great. Punters are rolling in. You should do well with your yellow bucket," he chortled.

The helter skelter was really in swing, dozens of children were queuing to get a mat and squeal down the ride. All ages were jumping off at the bottom, laughing, running and pleading for money to have another go.

I trundled around the ride towards the hot dog stall. Normally I would have inhaled all that lovely onion smell and the lure of sausages and burgers but today I felt sick with the smell and heat.

"Well Fred I do declare," shouted a voice from the stall. "What's doing with you lad?" Yet another chuckle and then laughter. "You keep going lad, you're doing fine." Benny was an old friend of Fred's.

"They do like their little jokes my pals," thought Fred gritting his teeth. If they only knew.

"Yep, thanks Benny, see you later in the pub, mine's a pint of cider."

"Yeah yeah," he joked back and mine's half a dozen eggs." With this, Benny rolled with laughter.

Fred thought to himself, "Just you wait mate, I'll get you back tonight. I'll put blackcurrant in his beer, he'll see!" He was making his way over to the "Quackers" stall for another well-earned sit down.

"Hiya Fred," said his girlfriend Becky. "How ya doing kid? You look great and the bucket is filling up nicely."

Before he could reply, a little boy and girl ran up to him and the girl promptly sat on his lap. He was so taken aback, he just let it happen. She was swinging her legs, chatting nine to the dozen

"Hey mister, what you doin' sitting 'ere?" she chirped, her neck stretching upwards to try and locate the mesh eyes.

"I'm not a mister," Fred retorted. "I'm the fairground's biggest duck, in fact I'm the biggest duck in the world." He stuck his chest out as far as he could and moved his wings in a kind of quacking movement.

"Coo, I can see that," said the little girl now known as Claire and her brother Joe. "You're lovely, really lovely and so fluffy. Can I take you home?" Claire wrapped her little arms around Fred's waist as far as she could.

"Oh 'eck," thought Fred, he stopped trying to puff out his chest and instead gently placed Claire on to the grass. He didn't feel gentle because he knew that he would have to head out again with his yellow bucket. Off he went.

"Nice one Fred," called the coconut shy stallholder. "Having much luck? It's certainly heaving now, the heat's enough to melt the ice-cream stall"!

"Tell me about it," whimpered Fred, who by now was sweating from his head down and felt that it was coming through his costume. "A rainfall or snow storm right now would help me immensely."

"Oh, come on Fred, you're doing great, everyone thinks so, so go get'em boy." Thus, spoke Fred's dad Barney. He thought his son a very brave soul on this sweltering day and, knowing everyone would be pulling his leg, he knew he would stick it out despite the down sides. He was a kind person and loved kids really.

Another hour passed. Fred was really wilting now. Three ice-creams, a smoothie, lemon drizzle cupcake from his favourite baker, his Mum's stall, who gave him a big hug and encouragement. He was finding it all a bit too much. He was hot, fed up and felt sick. He decided to turn around and head back for the stall, where at least he could take off his head and sit down in the shade.

119

Suddenly from nowhere about fifteen children from the helter skelter ran across the grounds and headed towards Fred. He was grabbed by the legs, around his waist, children shouting and hugging his fluffy body.

"Whoa, whoa there," shouted a worried Fred. He felt as if the bouncy castle had collapsed around him.

"We've been looking for you," tweeted a little girl of about six pushing her way to the front. Another little girl who had been pushed to the ground sat crying on the grass. Fred's heart went out to her, she started to sob. He found himself wondering if he could possibly gather her up with wings.

"Okay, here goes" he thought to himself.

Fred picked her up, she slipped a bit, but he shuffled her between his wings, his hands being able to hold her. Her mother ran up from the back of the group.

"What on earth is the matter Janey?" she whispered to her daughter, not wanting to bring publicity to the situation.

Janey slowed down the sobbing, which had now turned into a lot of sniffling.

"What's that on your head?" she managed to whimper.

Fred looked at all the faces looking up eagerly for his answer.

Suddenly Fred's calm slipped.

"I'm a duck, the largest duck in the world, get it.?" The day got to him and he yelled with wings wide open and as the children stood back in awe.

"Yes, we know that fluffy, but what's that thing on your head?" chirped Janey feeling safe in mum's arms.

Fred let it all out by yelling again, "What's that stall over there, all those poles and all those little yellow things swimming round that stall?"

Fifteen heads turned, along with some of the adults. Shoulders raised then fell as if in submission. As Fred sighed heavily and was about to give it his all, the other little girl suddenly realised what he was trying to say.

"It's Hook a Duck stall, Fluffy," she cried out with glee as if she had won a teddy bear on the ball stall.

"Exactly," shouted Fred, a bit of the stuffing knocked out of him. "Exactly, so guess who I am?" He looked at them defiantly.

"Aha." he thought to himself gleefully preparing for his crescendo.

"I'm HOOK, you know HOOK THE DUCK!!!!

They all stared, awe on their little faces. Out of the group, two children fought their way to the front, it was Claire and Joe.

"There you are, Fluffy" cooed Claire grabbing hold of his left wing. "They call you Fluffy, not Hook, and I asked me mam and she says I can take you home with us."

Fred groaned, the kids started to talk rapidly and as they grabbed him they were yelling that they all wanted to take him home. Fred had no control of the situation and fell to the ground as very ungraciously as one could in a large fluffy duck costume. Now there was such a crowd around him and everyone was helpless with laughter at the whole thing.

Fred's bucket was overflowing, so much so that another yellow bucket had to be brought to the scene by Becky, who brought her camera to capture this event. This would make fantastic headlines for "Quackers" and the carnival, and her beloved Fred would be a hero. She blew him a kiss, she could see his eyes widening and helpless under the mesh eyes.

"Bless him," she thought lovingly and laughingly. "At least he's my bit of fluff!!

Sea Glass

Sharon Brady-Smith

Waves pounded ruthlessly against the beach all night, whipped to a frenzy by the howling winds and rain. Although it was June the early morning temperature chilled blood and bone like mid-winter and the sky was fully as dark with its roiling grey clouds.

None of us had slept but, with low tide approaching we crawled, cold and exhausted, from beneath our threadbare blankets. Father's hollow cough sounded worse today. He should stay in bed, but we needed every hand to search for the bounty such wild nights delivered. The whole village would be there to gather their share to survive the winter ahead.

Cloaks drawn tightly against the elements, a torchlit procession of villagers walked single file down to the beach below. By unspoken agreement, Father carried the torch and held my elder brother's hand. I wondered again if we should leave Trevor here in the warm, but he would wander off. Worrying about him was once Mother's role and, as I harnessed Despair and hitched him to the cart, I felt her absence keenly.

We reached the parade of villagers and joined the tail. I sighed with relief when I realised how far back we were. Oldman Evans, the village leader, and his son Saul should be at the front. I wouldn't have to listen to him speak against mother and us, her fey get. Staring at the water, I fingered the sea glass token at my throat and wondered again if I would really be welcome with Mother's people as she once promised

Each family headed for their allocated section of beach. Ours was at the farthest end of the cove, past the sand and deep into the shingle. The short window of opportunity between tides ensured we had no time to neighbour. Heads down and shoulders bowed we started at the water's edge and worked back up the beach, combing for sea coal dredged from the ocean floor by the storm. Each deposit of the heavy wet coal we shovelled into sacks and loaded onto the low wagon. Despair trailing behind us unbidden as we worked.

Father spent as much time doubled over and coughing as he did shovelling. Only a year ago he could fill two sacks for each of mine, but now he barely worked at half my speed. My chest burned, my back ached, and my limbs trembled with the effort expended

Like me, Trevor never spoke. His other differences were more pronounced. He walked with the aid of a cripple's cane and wouldn't follow the simplest instructions. A man full grown but more childlike than a toddler, wandering to-and-fro as the whim took him and searching in rock pools. We had to watch him as well as the approaching tide. For the tide was a danger to us all until he found what he sought.

All too soon, the sky lightened, and the water licked at our toes. Our wagon was still half-empty, but we didn't dare stay any longer. Father turned to the rocks to call Trevor back, but he wasn't there.

I looked around me. The beach was already almost deserted. Most of the villagers had started their journey back up the path to their homes.

'Trevor.' He shouted, knowing Trevor wouldn't reply even if he could.

My stomach fell as my heart rose into my throat. We'd only turned away from him for a moment.

I ran to the outcrop where Trevor had been poking in a rock pool with his cane. His hat and cane lay discarded on the rocks, of my brother there was no sign. I studied the shingle, looking for indentations where he'd walked. Rocks held secrets better than sand.

I craned back my head and scoured the cliffs. Though Trevor's deformity hindered him walking, it had never slowed him down when he climbed. The sun rose from behind the cliffs, even now they were in full shadow and Trevor would only be a patch of movement. Nothing. It was a slight hope.

'I'll take the cart back and check he's not followed any of the others. Walk the beach a bit,' he said, gathering the harness. 'Whatever happens girl remember, I love you.'

I nodded and, on an impulse, hugged him as he turned to walk away. Despair was the only one to look back.

Everybody knows the stories. Once upon a time, a man found a selkie's skin and hid it from her, claiming her as his wife until she found her skin and left in the night.

Some stories are true, but the grey seals would no longer come if Father were on the beach. It broke his heart, but it was his own fault. What he'd done was wrong, but he loved my Mother still.

She'd been a good wife and bore him two children. The children were neither human nor selkie, lacking the skins to become seals.

Their first transition needs a token from the sea, one which calls only to them, and the aid of a selkie.

I could have left already. I wore a sea glass pendant on a thong about my neck, but Trevor had never found his. Until today. It hurt he hadn't even bothered to show me before he left.

Clutching the pendant tightly in my palm, I began to sing the song of my mother. My voice, haunting and inhuman, my mother's gift and the reason folk thought me mute. With Father gone, she came with her selkie family and my missing brother.

They both sang for me. 'Join us. Heed the sea's call and leave the shore behind.' The waves lapped at my ankles and I ached to go to them. But now I knew Trevor was safe I had to follow my father. I would join them one day, but I couldn't leave father all alone.

Despair waited for me in the yard, still hitched to the cart. I'd never known Father to neglect him this way. I cared for our horse, but I didn't bother to unload the cart.

He had taken to his bed without even learning of Trevor's fate. 'With your mother?' Father stated more than asked as he shivered beneath his sheets.

When I nodded, he wept and aged a decade in an instant, becoming old and frail before my eyes. Intuition told me Despair and I would both find new homes in the morning.

I heaped precious coals in the fireplace and settled down to wait for the end of Father's story. As I watched the sea coal flames burn blue for possibly the last time, I sang the song which snared my father. In his sleep Father smiled.

A Drop of Blood

Penny Wragg

The irregular splotches of blood on the blue linoleum started him chuckling again. What a stupid thing to do - to drop the piece of lambs' liver he'd bought for his supper. He was looking forward to frying it with some onions and a rasher of bacon. He scraped it up as best he could, but the residue looked like a murder had taken place. What would Elsie think when she came in to clean in the morning? Never mind, it would give her something to talk about other than her varicose veins or latest trip to see her gynaecologist. Suddenly he had a brilliant idea! He would leave her a note before he went to the office. He found a scrap of paper and wrote:

> *"Dear Elsie, I am leaving the country because I've murdered my wife. Please clean the floor as best you can. Sorry about the mess. Could you carry on coming as usual? I've hidden the body where it won't be found for a long time. Please don't talk to the police. Sincerely, Jason."*

♦ ♦ ♦

She'd always enjoyed going to her 'Am Dram' society and had played various roles from wronged wife to grumpy char lady and detective. Did it take up too much of her time? Did her husband feel neglected? It was like the family she never had, and it was fun. Halfway through Scene 3 of the rehearsal she realised she'd left her watch and the money she owed Jane for the Christmas meal on the worktop. It had to be in tonight. If she nipped back now she could be back for Act 2. She explained to the others and set off in her smart new blue Octavia.

♦ ♦ ♦

Jason put the note on the worktop. "There's a surprise for Elsie in the morning," he thought. He heard his wife's car outside. Well –

127

earlier than usual! He had to get his own supper more often than not. Then she was on her laptop all evening – no company at all. Would things have been different if they'd had children? He might as well be on his own. Come to think of it, that was a tempting prospect…

♦ ♦ ♦

Frank had suffered from depression for most of his life. He had learned to live with the ups and downs. Now they called it bi-polar disorder. It didn't help to have a label. It was just how he was. Elsie understood how it was for him. He had some periods when he felt positive and creative so joining the local art group had helped. Elsie had encouraged him to frame one of his pictures and hang it on the living room wall: the one of Sheffield's last tram which he'd seen at Crich tramway museum. He was glad she had her cleaning jobs and her own friends and interests. He didn't mind being on his own as long as he knew when she was coming home. He'd be lost without her.

♦ ♦ ♦

Jason experienced a moment of madness. The gleaming kitchen knife lay on the table. It flashed into his line of vision as if saying tantalizingly, "Use me." He turned the lights off.

♦ ♦ ♦

'Good job I've got my door key,' she thought, letting herself in quietly. She didn't bother to put the light on. She intended just to grab her watch and the envelope and get back quickly. She had seen Jason's red Audi in the drive but didn't want to disturb him. He worked hard and was tired in the evenings. As she reached out towards the worktop she heard someone behind her. A strong arm squeezed her around the neck. She couldn't shout out. She couldn't breathe. She glimpsed a flash of silver as a cold sharp blade plunged into her throat and she knew nothing but blackness.

♦ ♦ ♦

Samantha finally switched off her computer, picked up her briefcase and locked the office. It was getting a bit much, this working overtime. Hopefully, they could close the deal with the Canadians within the month. She enjoyed her work but it didn't help her marriage. She knew her husband resented the fact that she put her job before him. It was a great sadness to them both that they hadn't been able to have a family. Focusing on her work had helped although she supposed it was a bit unfair to expect him to cook his own supper every evening. He was becoming crabby and his behaviour was slightly erratic. It took twenty minutes to drive home. She was about to park her white Punto outside the house when she noticed a familiar blue Octavia in her usual space.

◆ ◆ ◆

On arriving home, Jane, that stalwart of the "Am Dram" society, wondered why Elsie hadn't returned to the rehearsal. She was usually so conscientious. Perhaps she'd changed her mind and gone home early. Although she had said that she'd only be fifteen minutes. The phone was ringing as she entered the hall. It was Elsie's husband, Frank, who she knew quite well. He was in rather a state. He sounded agitated, asking where Elsie was. He expected her home by now. He couldn't remember how to make his bedtime cocoa. Jane tried to pacify him saying that Elsie would be home soon, although she had to admit to herself that she felt uneasy.

◆ ◆ ◆

Samantha wondered why all the lights were out and why Elsie's car was here as she only came two mornings a week. She switched on the kitchen light and screamed, then gagged at the amount of red blood on the blue linoleum and the sight of Elsie's body. Jason was sitting by the fridge. He seemed completely out of it. The only thing Samantha could think to do was go around and break the news to Frank that Elsie wouldn't be coming home – ever.

◆ ◆ ◆

Frank was in a terrible state. He couldn't see properly. The blackness had descended. How dare Elsie be so late? She knew he couldn't cope on his own. She didn't deserve the new blue Octavia which he'd bought for her. Through a haze, he heard a knocking at

129

the door. Had she forgotten her key? He opened the door and she started to speak, "Oh Frank…" He saw a red mist. He was overcome by a superhuman force which was outside his control. He put his hands around her neck and pulled tight on her scarf. Funny, he didn't remember this orange one. She struggled hard, but he didn't let go.

♦ ♦ ♦

Jason didn't know what had happened. There was a body on the kitchen floor. It should have been Samantha, but it was Elsie their cleaning lady – dear old Elsie. He dialled 999.

♦ ♦ ♦

And there, dear reader, we leave them. The police will have many threads to untangle, I fear. At one house they will find a man in total shock who appears to have murdered his cleaning lady by stabbing her with a kitchen knife, but he has written a note confessing to the murder of his wife. A few streets away they will find the body of a young woman who they will later identify as the aforesaid wife. She has been strangled by an older man who is now barely conscious, having taken an overdose of anti-depressants. Who will drive the brand new blue Octavia now? And who will clean the blue linoleum?

Author Biographies

In alphabetical order:

Sue Allott

(The Dragonfly, Hook the Duck)

Diane Bingham

(Que Calor!)

P J Bird

(The Story of a Bear)

Sharon Brady-Smith

(The LWC and Damned by 'I Do.', Sea Glass)

Bob Mynors

(STANNINGTON NOIR: You Don't Need a Weatherman to Know Which Way the Wind Blows, Spring Fervour)

Carol Ritson

(Wayfinders, Wise Woman of the Dreamtime, Warrior Women, Death Wish)

Phil Warhurst

(Danger at Ramsey Manor)

Penny Wragg

(Clarissa's Party, After the Earthquake, A Drop of Blood)

Susan Allott

Susan Allott lives with her husband in Stannington and joined the Stannington Library Writers' group during 2016. Writing is a relatively new accomplishment for her, which she must fit around all her other community commitments.

She is an active member of Knowle Top Methodist Church, and she helps to organise their many events which, mostly, keeps her out of mischief. She still finds time for her friends, and fortunately for this anthology as well.

'Susan has previously published stories in the 2016 Christmas Anthology and the nXstannthology.

Diane Bingham

I have been researching my family history for many years and the more I find out about my genealogical tree, the more I become interested in the context in which my ancestors lived: the social history. For example, not just where my French ancestor was during the Napoleonic Wars – he was a POW in Bristol - but the society into which he was released, with all those displaced returning soldiers. Knowledge of history aids family history research – we find out about the existence of muster rolls and hearth tax records - and knowledge of our family history helps us witness the impact of historical and political events on the society of the time. I am seeking a way to understand and appreciate the lives of my ancestors, not just the bare facts of their existence.

P J Bird

Patrick Jonah (P. J.) Bird is the altogether more intriguing alter-ego of one Matthew Lowson.

A keen writer for the better part of eleven years, Matthew has previously contributed to the anthology 'Tales from the Library'.

As half of the writing duo 'Bird and Marks' Matthew has co-written, co-produced and indeed performed in a series of murder mystery plays entitled 'Murder at Mauderville Manor'. The effect of which has led to audiences turning into sleuths for an evening without the need for a deerstalker. These evenings have raised funds for different charities.

Hailing from Steel City, Matthew is a Blades supporter and works as a Mathematics Champion Teaching Assistant at a local primary school.

Sharon Brady-Smith

Sharon Brady-Smith is the pseudonym for Sharon Smith, as there are too many of them. She is happily married with two grown up children, Laura and Bryan, and a spoilt fur baby called Cookie.

Sharon leads writer's groups based at Ecclesfield and Stannington libraries in Sheffield, England where she lives Her first solo book was self-published in 2016, a short story collection called "Sharon's Shorts". She publishes the Writing Group's anthologies. She also volunteers for several local community groups and when she has the time, she reads speculative fiction and urban fantasy romance.

https://sharonbradysmith.wordpress.com/

Bob Mynors

Bob Mynors was born in Sheffield, England, in October 1951. Keen to have no time to watch telly ever again, working hard to try and write as funny as The Bonzo Dog Doodah Band played, he is committed to eradicating full stops at ends of paragraphs

"You know when the paragraph has ended: there are no more words left to read till the next one starts. If all the full stops at the end of all the paragraphs ever printed in the world were not there, think how much ink would be saved

"I'm just doing my bit."

He published his first solo anthology, 'Fake Histories', in 2018 and has contributed to both Stannington and Ecclesfield Library Writers Groups' anthologies

Carol Ritson

Carol grew up in Hillsborough and has lived in Stannington for twenty-nine years.

For a while, she wrote the "Meeting people" articles for the monthly Parish Magazine; an idea which has more recently been revived as a similar 'interview style' article in the new quarterly Stannington Parish Magazine.

Having not written fiction since her school days she joined the Stannington Writers Group three years ago and has since had work published in both the 1stannthology and the 2017 Christmas Anthology.

She is a lover of music, art, nature, crafts, maths and science. She is sociable, talkative, geeky, enjoys meeting new people and can more often than not be found in coffee shops chatting and laughing with friends.

Phil Warhurst

Born in 1960 Phil worked in Sheffield schools for over 30 years teaching English and Drama. He finally completed his probationary period in 2017.

He has been involved with Amateur theatre even longer than teaching and currently plies his trade with Hallam 89 Theatre Club, a company he helped set up in 1989, surprisingly enough.

A keen Owls supporter he has paused going to see the matches partly because of, ironically, the poor amateur dramatics of the players and the desperate need of the footballers to swap shirts ages before the final whistle.

Having spent many hours trying to teach others how to be creative in writing and performing he thought it about time he taught himself to do the same.

Penny Wragg

Penny is Sheffield born and bred and proud of it! She has lived in Stannington for 38 years and is a member of Christchurch.

She has always loved writing and was thrilled to have a poem published in her junior school magazine when she was nine.

She claims to be well known in some circles for writing "odes" for people on special occasions. However, at the moment she is enjoying writing about her memories of growing up. Penny says, "I find this therapeutic and I hope that some of my words will live on after me!"

In memory of my Dad who loved books

and my Mum who sent me to elocution lessons.

36005810R00088

Printed in Great Britain
by Amazon

LATESTANNTHOLOGY

Short Story Anthology 2018

Stannington Library Writers' Group

LATESTANNTHOLOGY

Short Story Anthology 2018

Stannington Library Writers' Group

Also by Stannington Library Writers Group

1stannthology

nXstannthology

Christmas Anthology 2016

In association with

Ecclesfield Library Writers Group

Christmas Anthology 2017